I0587527

Janelle Reston's
Best Lesbian Erotica
From Sweet to Spicy

HOT DRINKS PRESS · STORIES TO SAVOR

©2018 by Janelle Reston

All rights reserved. No part of this book may be reproduced or transmitted in any form or by any means, electronic or mechanical, including photocopying, recording, or by any information storage and retrieval system without the written permission of the publisher, except in the case of brief quotations embodied in critical reviews and certain other noncommercial purposes permitted by copyright law. To request permission and all other inquiries, contact Janelle Reston via www.janellereston.com.

"Dance for Me" by Janelle Reston ©2016, 2018. First published in *From Top to Bottom* by LadyLit Publishing, April 2016.

"Water & Air" by Janelle Reston ©2015, 2017, 2018. First published in *Like a Spell: Volume One* by Circlet Press, Cambridge, MA, 2017.

"Wordless Surrender" by Janelle Reston ©2016, 2018. First published in *Best Women's Erotica of the Year, Volume 2* by Cleis Press, 2016.

"Bicycling Puts the Fun Between Your Legs" by Janelle Reston ©2016, 2018 First published in *Best Lesbian Erotica of the Year, Volume 2* by Cleis Press, 2018.

"An Amish Girl Experiments with Chemistry" by Janelle Reston ©2016, 2018. Revised version of a story first published in *Love Slave: Sizzle* by Lit Select, 2016.

"Making Snow" by Janelle Reston ©2016, 2018. First published in *Lustily Ever After* by A Two Dame Production, 2016.

"In a Pinch" by Janelle Reston ©2016, 2018. First published in *Unspeakable Erotic: Lesbian Kink*, Cleis Press 2017.

"Body Shots" by Janelle Reston ©2015, 2016, 2018. First published in *Girls on Campus* by Bold Strokes Books, 2016.

"Alien Vibes" by Janelle Reston ©2015, 2018. An earlier version of this story was published in *The First Annual Geeky Kink Anthology* from Riverdale Ave in November 2015. Please do not purchase the Riverdale Ave anthology, as Janelle was never paid for her contribution despite numerous attempts to remedy the issue with the publisher. To Janelle's knowledge, the editor and other contributors also went unpaid.

This is a work of fiction. Names, characters, places, and incidents either are the product of the author's imagination or are used fictitiously. Any resemblance to actual persons, living or dead, is entirely coincidental. All persons depicted on the cover are models used for illustrative purposes only. All trademarks and wordmarks used in this collection of fiction are the property of their respective owners.

Cover image by Engin Akyurt.
First edition.
Published in the United States by Hot Drinks Press.
Trade paper ISBN: 978-1-64231-004-7
Ebook ISBN: 978-1-64231-002-3

Table of Contents

About the Stories

Body Shots
A first-year college student goes wild at a party thrown by the women's rugby team.
Exhibitionism, semi-public sex

An Amish Girl Experiments with Chemistry
Rachel Yoder has discarded her drab Amish garb for hot pink short-shorts, but she hasn't forgotten what she learned growing up—love is expressed through baking. Her assistant Leticia wants to taste more of Rachel's love than sweet rolls can provide.
Sex at work, masturbation, masturbation with sex toys

Bicycling Puts the Fun Between Your Legs
Two women experience lust—and maybe love—on a long-distance bike ride through New Jersey's Pine Barren's to the Atlantic shore.
Shower sex

Water & Air

Miranda is an ordinary young woman resentful of the magic that runs in her family but has skipped her generation. If she had such powers, she certainly wouldn't be like the witches who descend on her lake resort town every summer, wasting their powers on stupid party tricks.

But when Miranda meets a water witch named Hazel, she starts to wonder if the practitioners of magic aren't so bad after all. And if reconciling herself to the world of witchcraft means she has a better chance of sleeping with Hazel, well, so much the better.

Outdoor sex, improvisational sex toys

Making Snow

In this sexy, modern take on the Grimm fairy tale "Frau Holle" ("Mother Hulda"), a ski resort manager falls through the ice and finds herself in a new world of sensual delights.

Masturbation, voyeurism, exhibitionism

Dance for Me

Myra Jamison's submissive tendencies awaken under the rigorous teaching methods of dance professor Hannah Lacey. But Myra soon discovers not any Domme will do. Only Professor Lacey knows how to break Myra down, then make her more whole than she was before.

Masturbation, light BDSM, restraints, improvisational sex toys

In a Pinch
Grad students Jess and Nicole have always had a pretty vanilla sex life. That all changes when Nicole overhears Jess making strange sounds behind a closed door.
Sex toys, pain play

Alien Vibes
A couple's obsession with *The X-Files* and little gray aliens goes deeper than most.
BDSM role play, abduction fantasy, restraints, medicalized sex play, customized sex toys, enjoyable anal penetration

Wordless Surrender
A Deaf dominant plays with the submissive female partner of her dreams. *All About Romance* says this story "has an extremely strong sense of character alongside a rapturous sense of love for bondage and dominance that translates well even if you don't kink to it."
BDSM, sensory deprivation, restraints, sex toys

Body Shots

I SELECTED A WOMEN'S COLLEGE for one reason: I was desperate to get laid.

After all, my high school counselor had practically guaranteed it would happen. Well, okay—those weren't his *exact* words. When he asked me to name the colleges I was thinking about and Smith, Mount Holyoke and Sweet Briar came up on the list, he said, "Don't you know those are girls' schools?"

I nodded. Some of my friends thought it was weird, but it wasn't like I needed boys around. I wasn't interested in fucking them.

He cleared his throat. "Only lesbians go to girls' schools, Madison," he said, then hedged. "Except maybe Sweet Briar. Lots of Southern belles there. I don't think Southern belles can be lesbians."

That decided it. I crossed the coed schools from my list and focused on women's colleges north of the Mason-Dixon line.

College was going to be great. I'd hook up with my roommate. We'd invite the whole hall over for nightly orgies. Sure, I'd go to classes and do my homework, but the rest of it would be one big blur of lesbian sex.

My counselor, it turned out, was misinformed. Within three hours of arriving on campus, I found out more than half my hallmates had off-campus boyfriends. My roommate plastered her side of the room with pictures of Zac Efron, Chris Evans, and Harry Styles. Obviously, a girl can be queer and still like men, but that was not the case with her.

Fortunately, there was also Frankie.

It was the second week of school and I was in one of the private shower enclosures, singing to myself—a habit I hadn't managed to break yet even though I was now sharing a bathroom with thirty near-strangers. Halfway into the song, I realized my voice wasn't alone. Someone had joined in with a rich, silky harmony that echoed pleasantly against the tiles.

"Who's that?" I said, peering out from behind the curtain. A tiny woman in glitter eye shadow and a swirl-patterned minidress was standing at the sinks, a toothbrush hanging from her mouth. Her hair was in a haphazard knot on top of her head.

"Sorry," she said, still brushing. Her mouth was foaming with paste, but somehow she managed to look cute anyway. "I didn't mean to interrupt you."

"You didn't. I just wanted to know—well, you

have a nice voice." She was too adorable to be real. I wondered if she was some kind of siren, seducing unsuspecting first-years with impromptu duets. I wouldn't have minded. Unless—"You're not trying to recruit me to an a cappella group, are you? Or have I stumbled onto the set of *Pitch Perfect*?"

She spat into the sink. "Absolutely not. I just sing when I feel like it. Rugby's my thing."

That was a jolt. "No offense, but you don't look like a rugby player." Even though her arms were as buff as Michelle Obama's, it was hard to imagine her petite bones were much thicker than a bird's.

She laughed. "People like me can squeeze through those big piles of players."

We started hanging out a little, sitting at the same table in the dining hall or doing impromptu duets in the dorm living room. I asked her if she was into girls.

She laughed and set down her french fries. "Are you asking me that because I'm a rugby player?"

"No," I said. "I'm asking because ... I'm asking." That wasn't the truth. I was asking because I had a huge-ass crush on her, but I didn't have the gonads to say so.

"Fair enough. I've been intimate with women," she said, then gave me a sly look, "and I'd like to be intimate with a woman again."

That sly look haunted me. Was she flirting with me? Was she implying that it was *me* she wanted to be intimate with? I thought about it a lot the next few days. I also thought about her fingers, her voice, her pert little ass. I thought about what her body might feel like over or under mine, how her lips would feel on my throat, how her tongue would feel between my legs. I wore the batteries in my vibrator out.

That weekend, she invited me to a post-game rugby party.

"Aren't those just for the players?" I said.

"Nah," she said. "We can bring as many guests as we want."

As many guests as we want probably meant this was not a date, but I dressed my casual best anyway, choosing a sexy-cute fitted shirt and shorts. Underneath I wore my favorite bra and thong panties—a black silky set with tiny brass accents on the hips and cleavage. I didn't set my hopes on revealing them to Frankie, but they made me feel more confident in my skin.

Frankie knocked on my door at 9 p.m. She was wearing a sleeveless black minidress that would have made her look like Audrey Hepburn if it hadn't been made of vinyl. It clung to her every curve: shapely hips and ass, muscular thighs, and breasts just the right size to fit completely in my hands. There was a long zipper that went up the front, with a pull-tab shaped like an arrow. It pointed straight up to her cleavage. I tried not to stare.

I assumed there'd be a whole group of us walking over, but it was just us. Maybe this *was* a date. We walked close to each other as we crossed the campus, our hands sometimes brushing as we moved along. I became aware of my thong shifting against my labia and asshole with each step. By the time we got to our destination, my panties were thoroughly wet.

The party was in the common room of one of the older dorms. It had a wooden floor and a ceiling that must have been twenty feet high, with tall leaded glass windows that looked like they belonged in a church. When she walked in a loud cheer of "Frankie!" went up and echoed against the stone ceiling.

I followed Frankie like a smitten puppy to a cluster of couches and sat down next to her, trying to follow the lively conversation about scrums, blood bins, grubber kicks, and face balls. Frankie served as my translator, leaning in to whisper explanations of what was being said without interrupting the flow of conversation. Her voice sounded lush and intimate, like she was reading love poems to me rather than explaining sports terms. At one point I thought I felt her lips brush against my ear. My nipples went hard from arousal. I almost moaned.

Once I was familiar with the jargon, Frankie turned away from me to join back in with the main conversation. But she stayed sitting just as close, setting her hand on my thigh as if she was trying to keep our connection. It wasn't in an indecent spot, exactly—maybe about a third of the way up from my knee, just below the hem of my shorts. But every once in a while she'd absentmindedly brush her fingertips back and forth along my skin—tiny movements, really, not more than a few millimeters. Still, each one felt monumental to me. I couldn't help wondering what it would be like if she touched my clit that way. Or better yet, what it would be like for *me* to touch *her* clit that way. Would she moan? Would she grind into my hand and cry out my name? Or was she a quiet lover whose arousal was told in low, gasping breaths?

I imagined myself between her legs, tongue lapping at her labia, her fingers in my hair. Her hands would coax me gently, guiding me to the places where my attention gave her the most pleasure, showing me how to bring her to higher and higher levels of ecstasy. What would she want me to do to her? Nibble at her clit? Curl my tongue into her cunt and lick at her sensitive walls? Move down further to bathe her delicate pucker in my saliva and her desire? I wanted to do all of it, and more.

Frankie's voice brought me back to the moment: both of us fully clothed, on a couch in a common room, surrounded by people. "Body shots!" she shouted. "That's a great idea!"

I had no idea what she was talking about. I assumed it had to do with rugby. All I knew was that I was so drenched in arousal that my thong couldn't hold it all. It had flooded the fabric, spreading to the insides of my thighs and down my ass crack.

Frankie turned to me. "You game, Madison?"

"Sure, when I get back." I said, still clueless about what I was agreeing to. "I just need to run to the bathroom."

I did so, cleaning myself up as best I could. If I'd had any sense, I would have jerked off while I was in there to diffuse the building tension in my body. But I didn't want to. I was enjoying my state of high arousal and the way it made my skin buzz.

When I got back, the party had transformed to a much more raucous affair. Frankie lay supine on a table, a glass of tequila on her pelvis and a lime wedge perched pulp-side-out between her teeth. An upperclasswoman stood over her, sprinkling salt from a shaker between Frankie's breasts. An electric energy sparked between them. The rest of the partygoers shouted encouragement.

I froze in my tracks, taking in the scene. Call me naive, but it took me a minute to figure out what was going on. I didn't party in high school, and this was one of my first parties at college. The dynamic between Frankie and the other woman looked so intimate it was almost unbearable to watch, but I couldn't have turned away even if I'd wanted to. Frankie was a magnet to my eyes.

"Do it, Shawnda!" someone hollered. The upperclasswoman bent low over Frankie, tonguing her salted cleavage. Frankie squirmed and gasped. She let out a delighted giggle. Her face and collarbone went pink.

My clit throbbed.

Shawnda then worked down Frankie's zipper to slurp the tequila out of the shot glass perched just above Frankie's snatch. When Shawnda had about half the tequila out of the glass, she pushed her tongue in to lap up the rest. Frankie's nipples went hard, visible like pebbles through the vinyl of her dress.

My trip to the restroom had been pointless. I gushed again. I shifted my legs and the thong moved over my labia in a frictionless glide. It felt amazing, so I kept shifting my legs—back and forth, back and forth as Shawnda licked every last drop of tequila from the symbolic orifice.

If I thought the tequila-drinking was hot, I had another thing coming. Shawnda crawled up Frankie's body and tongued at the lime wedge held in Frankie's lips, sweet tight circles and then tiny nips. I figured the next thing to happen would be Frankie spitting out the lime wedge for a real kiss that would turn into hard-core lesbian porn right before our eyes.

Or maybe that's what I was hoping for.

But it ended. Shawnda yanked out the lime wedge with her teeth and stood up with raised fists like she'd just made a touchdown—or whatever it is they call it in rugby. Frankie jumped up to receive the applause of a cheering throng, and the two women gave each other high fives and smacked each other on the ass like football buddies.

"I'm so turned on right now!" Frankie shouted. "And I know whose hot body I want to lick!"

"Frankie's choice! Frankie's choice!" the throng shouted in unison.

Her eyes scanned the crowd. As soon as she met my eyes, she pointed at me and licked her lips. "You're the one."

My breath caught in my throat. Frankie made a little come-hither motion with her index finger, though she might as well have been reeling me in on a fishing line, as incapable as I was of resisting her wishes. I walked toward her and lay down on the table, my breasts heaving in anticipation.

She bent over and whispered in the same intimate tone she'd used earlier, "You done body shots before?"

I shook my head.

"You don't have to, if you don't want to."

"I want to." There was a pang of desperation in my voice. Good. I needed her to know what she was doing to me.

She smiled. "There are two ways to do the tequila. I can put it in a shot glass and set it on your stomach, and then drink out of it. Or, you can pull up your shirt and I can drink it out of your belly button."

If words alone were capable of making me come, those words certainly would have done it. I closed my eyes and took a deep breath. I grabbed the hem of my shirt and pulled it up to reveal my belly and the low-cut waist of my shorts.

"Beautiful," she said. "Now the salt can go anywhere. Do you have a preference?"

I couldn't think of anywhere that I didn't want her tongue. I shook my head.

"I'm going to have my way with you now, Madison." And then she added, her voice low enough so only I could hear, "I've wanted to have my way with you for a while."

She popped the lime wedge into my mouth and I lay there, willing myself not to moan as she started her work. The tops of my breasts barely peeked out of my shirt, but she licked every bit she could manage, sprinkled me with salt, and then licked me again. I'd been to second base before but this was something altogether different, and hotter, with so many eyes on me and the cool tickle of salt contrasting with the warm tickle of her tongue.

I swallowed a whimper.

She licked up higher, up along my collarbone and neck, sprinkling trails of salt as she went. "Want to lick your thighs next," she murmured into my ear.

I groaned around the lime, nodding eagerly.

Frankie walked over to the far end of the table, positioning herself between my feet. She started at my ankle, with little nips and kisses up my calf that became more open-mouthed and wet as she approached my knee. The spectators went wild as she licked just above it on the inside of my thigh. They hooted and hollered and shouted her name. But none of their exuberance could match how I felt, seeing and feeling this gorgeous woman in such an intimate pose with me. She was close enough to my cunt that she could probably smell my arousal. I gushed a bit more at the thought.

Soon she was at my belly, pushing up the hem of my shirt, her hands ghosting over my skin. Someone handed her the bottle. She tipped it gently. A slow, thin stream trickled into my navel. I had masturbated in the shower before, aroused by the rush of water against my skin. This was something like that, only more refined and delicate—the difference between using a vibrator to buzz the whole of my snatch, or focusing its attention on the hardening nub of my clitoris.

The tequila filled my navel and spread across my belly. I sucked in my stomach to keep the liquid from dripping down my sides. She looked up at my face and licked her lips. "Now's where I get to pretend I'm eating you out," she said, and dove tongue first into the pool.

I bit hard into the lime. Juice squirted onto my cheeks. I closed my eyes and tensed my muscles, knowing that if I relaxed for just a moment I would lose all control.

Frankie continued laving me, her tongue everywhere on my belly, then dragging along my sides to chase droplets of tequila that had escaped. Cheers bounced off the stone walls and ceiling. Their vibrations felt like an impending orgasm. I squeezed my thighs together instinctively as Frankie licked the last drop of tequila from my skin.

But Frankie wasn't done with me yet. She crawled the rest of the way up my body and lowered herself on top of me, slotting her thigh between my legs as she sucked the juice from the lime. It took all my willpower not to hump against her, as hungry as I was to feel her heat between my legs.

Though my clit didn't get to touch her, my mouth finally did: She pulled the lime wedge from between my teeth, spat it to the floor, and began to kiss me in earnest—lips against lips, tongue against teeth, soft desperate moans mixing in the connected caves of our mouths.

At some point I became conscious of my name being chanted. Frankie became conscious of it, too. She pulled away, just enough so I could see her face as she spoke to me. "The way body shots usually go, it would usually be your turn to drink next."

I shook my head. "I don't want a drink. I want to fuck you."

"Good," she said, and kissed me again. "I want that too."

She stood up and took me with her, wrapping an arm around my waist as she announced over the boisterous crowd, "Madison is forfeiting her turn!" There was no shortage of catcalls as she pulled me out of the room.

We ran down the hall to the nearest bathroom and made a beeline for the showers. It was a full circle back to the way we'd met.

She tugged the shower curtain closed, undid my shorts and slipped her fingers under my thong before I even had her dress half-unzipped.

"Goddamn, you're wet." She bit my ear.

"I'm so close to coming already, I swear." I yanked down on the front of her bra, freeing a pert, round breast. Her nipple was hard as a rock. I sucked on it and she let out an airy moan.

She rubbed a finger lightly around my clit—not touching it, just teasing. "If I make you come now, do you think you can come again tonight?"

"I could come *all* night," I panted. "I'm so hot for you."

She kissed me fiercely then, all tongue and teeth, plunging into my mouth as she plunged her fingers into my hungry cunt. I grunted and spread, grinding into her hand as I grabbed at her zipper. "Need to touch you. Need to feel how wet you are."

Her dress fell open and she let it slide to the floor. It was a gorgeous sight. I ran my hands over her bare stomach and her delectable ass, pushed down her red panties to expose her soft bush. The hairs near her slit were drenched with her arousal, and she shuddered when I ran my finger over the wetness. I used my toes to pull her panties down the rest of the way to her ankles, and *oh* was that a delight, feeling the way her fingers shifted in my cunt, stroking across my G-spot as my leg rose and fell.

She stepped out of her panties and I raised my leg again, holding it up at the perfect angle by pressing my foot against the stall wall.

"Is this the spot?" she murmured, her breath hot in my ear as she stroked my G-spot again.

I couldn't answer. I just cried out, the sound echoing against the tile walls and concrete floor.

She looked proud of herself, but her pride turned to desperation as I parted her bush and ran my fingers over her swollen labia. She shivered and spread her legs, moving closer. "Need you everywhere," she said. She led my hand around to her voluptuous backside, down the narrow furrow of her crack. When I touched her asshole, her body jolted. "Yeah, right there," she said. "You have me so close." She straddled my thigh, spreading her lips against my skin and drenching me in her arousal. She was so wet and silky against my leg, and I swore I felt her clit swell more with each roll of her hips. She rocked back and forth, working my finger into her hot, tight hole.

"I want to taste you," I moaned into her mouth. "I want to lick your cunt and your ass the way you licked my belly."

She lost it then, grinding into me and gushing onto my thigh, warm and slick with the faintest smell of honey. She fucked against me and kept coming, jerking her fingers deep into me with each wave that rolled through her body. I bit her shoulder to keep from shouting again as I came. Against my closed eyelids I saw shocks of bright white light.

We collapsed against the wall, our chests heaving. Slowly, I became aware of our surroundings: the clinical tile walls, the shush-shush of running water in the shower stall next to us. She wrapped her arms around me and held me close. She kissed up and down my neck.

"Sleep over with me tonight?" she said. "My roommate's gone for the weekend."

"As long as you're not hell-bent on actually sleeping."

She laughed. "Not at all."

It was the beginning of a beautiful relationship.

An Amish Girl Experiments with Chemistry

RACHEL YODER WASN'T Amish anymore. She didn't wear a black bonnet over her hair or a navy blue dress that covered her body from wrist to neck to ankles, making her sweat heavily in the heat of a summer kitchen. She jotted down recipe notes on an iPad and rocked out to Sleater-Kinney and Beyoncé while baking. Her work clogs were a shimmery red patent leather that would never fly under her old community's *Ordnung*.

But she still preferred to bake the old-fashioned way, grinding fresh flour with a hand-powered burr mill and using whisks and wooden spoons instead of electric mixers. Despite owning a bakery smack in the center of downtown, nestled between a high-rise condo and the offices of an international software developer, she eschewed any modern conveniences that would decrease her physical contact with the ingredients. "Baking is like making love. The power in it comes from touch," she told her apprentice Leticia on their second day working together and in their third year of knowing each other. Leticia had been a regular customer since her senior year of college, in part for the food and in part because getting a glimpse of Rachel in her signature short-shorts always made her day brighter.

Rachel patted the dough with her palm. "Tools are fine when they act as an extension of your body. But when they replace your body, the connection gets lost."

"So you're okay with dildos, but not blow-up dolls?" Leticia had a habit of opening her mouth before thinking.

Not that Rachel would be shocked at the line of questioning. Two years after running away from her Amish settlement at seventeen, she took a job at a woman-owned sex toy store because it was the most un-Amish thing she could think of— intentionally seeking out orgasms, and sometimes using electricity to do so. Besides, it gave her the opportunity to catch up on everything she'd missed in her sheltered upbringing. She learned to be frank about everything.

Rachel laughed. "That's not a terrible way to paraphrase it, although my point was about baking, not about sex toys."

"Good. Because I'm never giving up my dildo."

Rachel blushed a bright pink that went all the

way to the roots of her light brown hair. She might be frank, but she was not without emotions. "Tease me all you want, as long as you remember that love makes everything taste better. And there's something that feels more honest to me when I use my hands at every stage of a food's creation. I hope it gives you the same sense of connection."

Rachel did more than lecture Leticia on her philosophy. She taught it in her every movement, in the way her forearm muscles clenched as she kneaded dough and her biceps bulged when she stirred vats of cake batter. She would sigh happily as if the work were some great pleasure, and soon Leticia found that it was. Whenever Leticia worked out the kinks in a piece of dough, it seemed to work out the kinks in her own body and emotions.

She wished she could touch Rachel the same way. Rachel's tank tops showed off her powerful arms, made that way through years of kneading dough by hand on her family's farm, then in the kitchen of her tiny apartment, and now here in the bakery for five years. Working on her feet had built endless legs with thighs as thick and juicy as Christmas hams, tapering at the knee before billowing out again into strong, curvaceous calves. The heat of the bakery allowed Rachel to show them off year-round. She had a collection of short shorts in bright colors that would have made her Amish bishop blush and cluck his tongue. That was half the fun of wearing them, Rachel said.

"Is that why you left? For short shorts?" Leticia said one Saturday morning three hours before sunrise as they prepared donuts for the indoor winter farmers market.

Rachel shook her head, dusting the counter with flour before turning out her bowl of dough. "No, they're just a bonus."

"Then why did you leave? I mean, it obviously wasn't so you could start using Cuisinarts."

"You honestly don't know?"

Leticia grabbed the donut cutters from a drawer. "I have a thousand guesses. I can't see you being happy in a place as restrictive as that. But what's the straw that broke the camel's back?"

"I can tell you that story. And then you'll tell me something about you?" Rachel's cool gray-blue eyes looked suddenly warm.

Heat pooled between Leticia's legs. "Anything you want to know."

"Good. I'll keep that in mind. Now start rolling your dough and I'll tell you a story."

Leticia turned out her bowl. They rolled their dough in synchronized strokes that matched the rhythm of the Gossip song playing in the background.

"Have you heard of *Rumspringa*?" Rachel said as the song faded out. The dough was the right thickness now, half an inch and springy.

Leticia dipped a cutter into the flour. "Nope."

"It's when the Amish teens go wild and get a

taste of modern life before deciding whether to become members of the church. Some kids get wilder than others, and some go so wild there's no turning back. That was me." Rachel was left-handed, and Leticia was right-handed. Their arms kept brushing together as they cut the donuts, sending frissons of want over Leticia's skin.

"Really? You wake up every day at 2 a.m. to make donuts. That hardly seems wild to me."

"Oh, but I was by Amish standards. Still am. Doesn't matter that I go to sleep before sunset and hate booze." Rachel leaned in and whispered conspiratorially, her breath hot against Leticia's ear. "You see, it was Joy Stoltzfus's pussy that made me finally realize the Amish woman's life of marriage and the white cap weren't for me. The taste of a woman is better than anything I can cook up."

"Wait? So you just fell into her lap and …?"

Rachel laughed. "No. It started with a game of spin the bottle. One thing led to another. Amish kids know how to party with the best of them. All that repression breeds recklessness."

"So what happened to this Joy Stoltzfus? Did she leave with you?"

"No. I don't think she was really gay. She only let me eat her out the one time, and a few months later she was on her way to getting baptized. But there were others. Let me tell you, there's nothing that feels quite so kinky as having your head and hands up an Amish girl's skirt. It was … *himmlish.*"

20

"*Himmlish?*"

"Heavenly. So much richer than the afterlife our preachers promised, that's for sure." Rachel sighed happily and squatted to pull a five-gallon jug of fryer oil from beneath the counter. Her short shorts clung to her shapely bottom as she spread her thighs to keep her balance.

"Let me help you with that." Leticia pulled on the jug's handle as Rachel lifted from beneath, their thighs touching as Rachel came to a full stand. She let out a soft grunt as they slid the heavy jug onto the counter—a low, primal sound that tingled down Leticia's spine and into her groin.

"Thanks." Rachel's collarbone and cheeks flushed from the exertion, and Leticia was reminded of sex again. Would Rachel blush ripe as a peach and make the same little groans if Leticia slipped her fingers up the inside hem of those short shorts and found the silken prize between Rachel's legs?

Leticia thought about this often as she worked, but she didn't do anything about it other than the occasional ambiguous flirtation. For her first few months at the bakery, she was trying to make a go of monogamy with a woman from her hockey league. In the weeks after they ended things, she figured it would be in good taste to make a show of being heartbroken.

She wasn't, though. Each hour away from that relationship was a step deeper into freedom, and maybe a step closer to getting into Rachel's shorts.

Leticia could hope, at least.

"Were you in love with her, Leticia?" It was two weeks after Leticia's break up. She and Rachel were piping strawberry jam into sugar buns.

"I wanted to be."

"But you weren't?"

Leticia looked up to study Rachel's face, but could only see the side of it. "No, I wasn't. I just thought … maybe it was time to get serious with someone. I won't be young forever."

Rachel glanced up then, laughing. "You're only twenty-seven—two years younger than me! If you were Amish, I could see why you'd think yourself an old maid. But we're out in the real world."

"I didn't say it made sense." Leticia shrugged. She felt light and giddy, the way she always did when Rachel laughed.

"No, I guess you didn't."

"Why do you ask, though? About whether I was in love?"

Rachel turned back to the pastries. "I thought maybe you could tell me what it's like, being in love. I've been with plenty of women and had my share of crushes, but sometimes I wonder—" She bit her bottom lip. "Never mind."

"You've never been in love?"

"I think … I've been on the edge of it." Rachel's ears went as red as cherry pie filling. "I've been infatuated, and I've had women who were

22

infatuated with me. But the chemistry has to be equally strong both ways for it to grow into something bigger, doesn't it?"

"Like yeast and sugar to make dough rise?"

Rachel scrunched her face. "I'd rather not mix yeast with my love-and-sex metaphors, if you know what I mean."

"Would baking soda and vinegar be better?"

"As long as we're making chocolate-vinegar cake and not douches."

Leticia burst out laughing.

The bakery kitchen had two counters: one in the center of the room and one next to the outside wall. When their work was too big to fit on one counter, Leticia took the table at the center of the room. "It's wobblier," she told Rachel. "You should have the good one since you spend more hours at this."

Leticia's real reason was less altruistic. Working at the center table gave her the perfect view of Rachel's backside. Leticia could spend hours happily staring at Rachel's pale neck, made bare by a loose chignon she usually held in place with a pair of gold-filigreed chopsticks. She loved studying Rachel's round ass and delicate ankles, and gazing at the backs of Rachel's knees. The muscles there formed shallow bowls that in spring had been the color of fresh cream. But in summer they darkened like ripening fruit, blushing apricot pink before mellowing out into the light beige of turbinado sugar—still pale in comparison to Leticia's muscovado brown.

Leticia wondered what the backs of Rachel's knees tasted like. Sweet as they looked, probably, and after a long day in the kitchen the flavor would undoubtedly be more complex, made piquant and salty from sweat and flour dust.

Leticia's fantasies became more detailed. She fantasized about the unseen parts of her boss's body, her pendulous Germanic breasts with nipples that could be small as dimes or large as Eisenhower dollars, her pubic area that might be shaved or covered with downy fur, her belly pale as milk, her labia pink as raspberries or brown as figs. As soon as Leticia got home from work she got into bed, working her butterfly dildo into her vagina and a butt plug the width of two fingers into her ass. She wrapped her thighs around a thick pillow, using the weight of her calves to thrust it against the toys, pushing them deeper into her body as she squeezed her breasts and stroked her belly, pretending the peaked nipples and the wetness gushing onto the pillow was Rachel's. She came with Rachel's name on her lips, her body shaking so hard even her skull seemed to vibrate.

She would have come even harder if she'd known Rachel was calling out her name just as eagerly from her bed a few blocks away.

Rachel stood at the counter by the wall, her back toward Leticia as she pummeled an unruly loaf into submission. The muscles of her arms and back rippled with each turn of the dough, and her thighs went tight, lax, and tight again.

Leticia imagined them squeezing around her waist as Rachel's wet, open vulva rubbed against her pubic bone, felt her own underwear growing slick from arousal. She worked her desire into the pastry before her, letting the large squares of lard and butter break into beads, squeezing the pliant dough the way she wanted to squeeze Rachel's shapely ass.

She would tell Rachel what she wanted soon, even if it meant risking her job. Or rather, she would tell Rachel as soon as she worked up the guts.

It was funny. Leticia wasn't shy, and she certainly wasn't a wimp. Why, then, did her stomach go all flippity-floppity whenever she thought of telling Rachel that she wanted her?

"Daydreaming again?"

Leticia looked up to find Rachel looking at her over her shoulder. Her pink lips were curled into a lopsided smile, and her blue-grey eyes sparkled. Heat rose to Leticia's cheeks. "Why? Did you say something?"

Rachel shook her head. Strands of hair fell loose from her chignon, sticking to the sweaty skin of her neck. "No. You're just so quiet sometimes. You used to talk more, when you first started working for me."

"Did I?"

"Almost non-stop." Rachel smiled affectionately and covered her dough with a large piece of damp muslin. She walked over to the center table, standing on the opposite side from Leticia. "I hope it's not because my Amish reticence made you feel like you had to stop being you."

Leticia laughed. "You? Reticent? I don't think so."

"So what is it?"

"Sometimes I talk a lot. And sometimes I get distracted by … the view." She patted the dough self-consciously.

Rachel furrowed her brows and glanced out the window. It overlooked a parking lot that looked gray in the early morning fog. "You call that a view?"

"No. That's not—That's not what I like to look at when I'm working." Leticia's errant eyes skimmed the curves of Rachel's torso.

"Oh," said Rachel—or not *oh* exactly, but the sound a breath makes when it catches in a person's throat. She coughed to clear it, then took another breath. She looked Leticia head-on. "Am *I* the view?"

Leticia's lungs went still mid-breath. She felt slightly dizzy, and a little drunk. She had the stupid urge to deny it, like when she was a kid and got caught sneaking panela from the pantry. But denial never helped in those situations, and it wouldn't help in this one. "Yes."

Rachel sucked in her bottom lip. "I think we should switch work stations."

"I'm sorry. I didn't mean to make you uncomfortable."

"You didn't. But I want to get a chance to enjoy the view, too." There it was again—the spark in Rachel's cool eyes. It grew into a flame as they dropped to Leticia's breasts, then hips.

Leticia's heart hammered in her ears. "You can do more than just look if you want." She leaned across the table toward Rachel, letting the low neck of her T-shirt slide down until she felt the breeze from the electric fans against the tops of her breasts.

Rachel's eyes followed the air current. Her fingers were next. She traced the skin along Leticia's neckline, stopping between her breasts. She licked her lips. "I'd love to. But we still have the order to fill."

Leticia glanced at the clock. "By my count, we're half an hour ahead."

Rachel crooked an eyebrow. "Half an hour? I'm not sure that would be long enough for all the things I've imagined doing to you."

"Then give me a small taste." Leticia closed the gap between them. Rachel's lips were slightly chapped, but soft, and tasted like the bakery smelled: flour and cinnamon, sugar and apricots. Beneath that there was the taste of human warmth and skin.

Rachel pulled herself onto the counter to get closer to Leticia, her knees barely missing the pastry dough. She let her clogs fall to the floor before sliding the rest of the way across the counter and over the edge, landing in Leticia's arms.

Leticia chuckled. "You must want me bad if you're willing to ruin your morning's work."

"You have no idea how turned on I get working with you. I've been wet since I got here."

"Oh yeah?" Leticia slipped her hand under the hem of Rachel's apron and up the seam of her jeans. "Are you going to let me feel?"

"If you want."

"You bet I want." Leticia pulled off Rachel's apron and her own, throwing them onto the counter. "And I thought my crush went one way."

"Nope. Definitely requited. I want to eat you for breakfast." Rachel sucked hard kisses to Leticia's collarbone and tackled the fly of her jeans, tugging them down with her panties. They fell around Leticia's ankles as she kissed around the manicured strip of black hair enveloping Leticia's mons. "That second day when you said you were never giving up your dildo—the image popped into my head of you getting fucked with one and I could never unsee it. Never *wanted* to unsee it. When I got out my own, I thought about sliding it inside you and making you come." Rachel parted Leticia's labia and gently licked from vagina to clit.

Leticia shuddered and curled her fingers into Rachel's hair, pulling more strands from its bun until the chopsticks came loose and went clattering to the floor. "I'm pretty sure I won't need a dildo if you keep doing that."

"Good, because I don't keep one in the bakery. I've got my hands, though, and fruits of all sizes and shapes." Rachel pushed a finger easily inside Leticia, curving the tip toward her belly and rubbing on the sensitive spot on the front of her vaginal wall. "You weren't kidding about being wet," Rachel whispered against Leticia's clit.

Leticia stepped out of her jeans and spread her legs. "I'd be even wetter if I got to touch you."

"Then come down here and go for it."

Leticia scrambled to the floor, kissing Rachel frantically as they tugged off shirts and bras and Rachel wriggled out of her hot pink short shorts. Leticia could taste herself on Rachel's mouth, sweet and musky like salted caramel. It made her mouth water for the taste of Rachel. She nudged Rachel's legs open and petted the dense fur between her thighs to each side, revealing the bright pink candy beneath. "How about we both have a little breakfast?" She sank her mouth to Rachel's clit and sucked until it grew into a hardened nub in her mouth.

Rachel gripped Leticia's head and cried out, her honey dripping onto Leticia's tongue.

"Not fair for you to have all the fun," Rachel moaned, then shifted to pull Leticia into a sixty-nine. Her breasts pressed against Leticia's stomach and her stomach against Leticia's hardened nipples as she kissed between Leticia's legs, pushing her tongue into Leticia's vagina with a hungry moan.

Leticia echoed the sound into Rachel's wet labia, and Rachel's cries grew louder and more desperate, each shock of pleasure traveling in a circular path through their bodies, vagina to spine to mouth and back to vagina again.

Leticia kneaded Rachel's plump ass and muscular thighs, and Rachel worked hers in turn, seeming to get as much pleasure from touching as she was from being touched.

Leticia remembered the words Rachel spoke on her second day at work: *Baking is like making love. The power in it comes from touch.* She felt Rachel's body more exquisitely, suddenly aware of every place where their skin made contact, unsure whether the pleasure that coursed through her was Rachel's or her own.

The hot flush of impending orgasm bloomed low between Leticia's hips. She tongued Rachel more desperately, deeply. An ecstatic wave crested through her body.

Rachel's flavor grew stronger—a heavy, sweet scent like beeswax and myrrh. She curled her fingers into Leticia's hips and thrust herself onto Leticia's tongue, her rhythm growing wilder as Leticia rubbed a thumb over her wet and swollen clit, the fingers of her other hand stroking the tight pucker of Rachel's ass.

"Du Gut in Himmel!" Rachel cried, biting Leticia's hip as her walls spasmed around Leticia's tongue and she gushed wetness onto Leticia's cheeks and chin. She arched and whimpered, then arched again.

Watching Rachel Yoder come was hotter than anything Leticia had ever imagined.

"Coomst du heer." Rachel pulled Leticia up to her mouth, kissing her until their flavors were so mixed Leticia couldn't remember one from the other.

"Is talking in Pennsylvania Dutch a good or bad sign?" Leticia asked, though she was pretty sure she knew the answer.

"The best sign." Rachel's chest heaved as she caught her breath. "It means I've come so hard I've forgotten what language I'm supposed to be speaking."

Leticia rubbed her nose against Rachel's flushed cheek. Her collarbone and stomach bloomed rosy, too. "What did you say?"

"Something like 'Dear God in heaven.' And then I told you to come closer to me."

"And how do you say 'more'?"

"*Mai.*' Why? You want more?"

"As much as you'll give me. I've got a pretty big crush on you. And the chemistry—" Leticia bit her tongue. She shouldn't show all her cards at once, no matter how head over heels she was.

Rachel gave her a knowing smile. "The chemistry works pretty well in both directions, doesn't it?"

Leticia let go of her tongue. "Yeah. I think it does."

Bicycling Puts the Fun Between Your Legs

"ALL THE NERVE ENDINGS in my crotch are officially dead," Morgan said as we rolled into the pit stop in New Jersey's Pine Barrens. Our cleats sank into the sandy soil as we dismounted our bicycles and propped them against the closest empty tree trunk. We were about halfway through our eighty-mile route from Philadelphia to the Atlantic shore, and the stop was already teeming with other cyclists taking a break.

In contrast to Morgan's, my crotch wasn't numb at all. It flushed practically every time I looked at her. My nerves down there felt as alive as ever, thank you very much.

I rubbed my palm over her bike saddle, still warm from her body. I felt slightly jealous that it got to spend so much time between her legs. "This seat isn't helping? You loved it at the shop." I'd gone shopping with her the previous week to help her pick it out. Morgan was fairly new to long-distance cycling and had complained about her previous saddle incessantly rubbing against her labia, and not in the good way. This new one was like mine, with a cutout to spare the delicate lady parts.

"It's not my labia that hurt. It's everything else." She pulled her empty water bottle from its cage and walked over to the drink tent a few paces away, removing the cap from the bottle to cram it full of ice.

Then, in full view of anyone who cared to look, she shoved the bottle down the front of her bike shorts, wriggled her hips to settle it between her thighs, and gave a little shiver of pleasure. "That's much better."

"Ice on your snatch? That's hard-core." I laughed even as I felt a quiver travel through my own hips. What I wouldn't have given to be that bottle.

"I told you it hurt. I feel like someone put a sledgehammer to my pussy, and not in a good way."

I was too hot from the pedaling to blush, but I ducked my head anyway as I filled my own bottles with Gatorade. "We should check the height and angle of your saddle then. A well-adjusted bike seat shouldn't make you feel like that."

She eyed me. "So your crotch is doing fine?"

"Never been better," I answered, still not

looking at her. I was afraid the double meaning would be evident in my eyes, and I wasn't sure I was ready for her to know how I felt about her— not until I could suss out her feelings. She was brash and a flirt, but she was like that with everyone, even dogs and the odd chickadee. I couldn't read too much into it.

We found a patch of bare dirt and sat down. "Mmmph, that's more like it," she muttered as she spread her legs open for a side stretch. "Nestles the ice right where I need it."

"Morgan, that can't be good for you. You're going to give yourself frostbite."

"You care about my cooch? That's so sweet of you." She tipped her head and winked at me. I felt my own cooch flush. Was she flirting? Or just being her usual brash self?

"I care about all of you. Seriously, I'm looking at your seat height before you get back on that thing."

She reached toward her other leg but kept her eye on me. "So you're telling me your crotch isn't bothering you at all after fifty miles?"

"A little tingly, maybe, but not in pain."

"Good tingly, or bad tingly?"

The fact of her asking made me all the tinglier. "For me to know and you to find out."

"Ooh, I bet it's the good tingly then."

"You know what they say: 'Bicycling puts the fun between your legs.'"

She snickered. "God, I wish."

I went to ask one of the pit stop volunteers for

some string. The guy found a spool of twine and gave me several feet. I brought it back to Morgan, who now lay flat on her back with her legs propped up against a tree trunk. Her water bottle had slipped forward so that it now bulged against the front of her shorts like a monster strap-on.

"Here, take that armadillo out of your pants. I need to take your measurements."

She looked up at me from her spot on the ground. "What for?"

"So I can adjust your seat."

"Don't I need to be on my bike for you to do that?"

"I wanted to spare you the pain for as long as possible."

She smiled with relief and sat up, whipping the water bottle out of her shorts and nestling against a tree root. "Have I told you lately how much I love you?"

She hadn't. I had never heard her utter the word 'love' in reference to anyone, unless you counted the times we'd talked about her realization that she hadn't really been in love with her ex. "No," I said. "But there's a first time for everything."

She looked right into my eyes. "Indeed, there is."

I held the string out to her. "Grab one end and hold it against your inseam. Then stretch out your leg."

She did as instructed, the tip of her index finger pressing down against her chamois, right where the opening between her labia would have been if she'd been naked. I tried not to think too much about that as I pulled the string taut and stretched it to the base of her foot. I crimped my end to mark off the right length. "Back in a flash."

"Uh-uh," she said. "I'm coming with you. I want to watch you in action."

"Think you'll learn a thing or two?"

"Oh, I know I will."

It took us a minute in the maze of trees to remember which one housed our bicycles, but we found them eventually. I took the emergency toolkit out of my saddlebag and used the string to check Morgan's seat height. "Holy crap, no wonder you felt like there was a sledgehammer on your snatch. This thing is at least an inch too high."

Her eyebrows shot up in surprise. "An inch makes that much of a difference?"

"You'll find out in just a second." I used my pocket Allen wrench to lower her seat. The nose was also tilted too far up, so I flattened it out to redistribute the pressure to her sit bones. "Here, get on and see how that feels."

She smirked. "That's what all the ladies say to me."

I held the bike steady as she mounted it and pedaled backward to test the feel of the seat without actually moving. "Oh my God. That's so much better. Here I thought my choice was between finishing the ride and obliterating my twat. But this is like … butter. Damn, I think my cunt might actually be usable by tonight."

There was no way I could avoid blushing this time. "Are you planning to use it?"

"I don't know. But I like to know it's an option. I guess we'll see what happens when we get to the shore, won't we?" She winked again.

We'd met earlier that summer on one of the training rides. It was my seventh year of long-distance cycling and her first, though she was a few years older than me. Despite the difference in our experience, our cadences were almost identical, so we kept ending up in the same pod of riders. Sometimes the pod dwindled to just the two of us. It was easy to find a rhythm with her and stay in it.

The training rides grew longer as the season progressed, and so did the time I spent with her. She was a great riding buddy, with a million stories to tell and the perfect amount of tough love when I wanted to toss my bike by the side of the road and sleep for the rest of the day—like the grueling 96-degree afternoon in August when she hopped off her bike only long enough to grab the sprinkler off someone's lawn and douse me with it. Her background was in marathon running, and those assholes never give up. A gaggle of nearby kids saw what she was doing and thought it was a hoot. They came running over and accosted us with water Uzis until both of our shirts were soaked through.

God, it felt good when we got back on our

bikes. The wind against the wet fabric worked like an air conditioner, and the way Morgan looked in her clinging jersey energized me even more. Normally white, it became almost transparent under these conditions. I could see her skin beneath it and the subtle movements of her back and arm muscles as she steered the bike. When she sat up to ride hands-free on the straight stretches, the outline of her pebbled nipples was unmistakable.

But just because two people have perfect cycling chemistry doesn't mean they'll fit together off the bike. Besides, Morgan had been on a dating sabbatical when I'd first met her, and I wasn't sure if it was over yet.

"How long do you think a person should go without sex after a bad break up?" she'd asked on our third ride together.

I liked to think she was wondering because of my irresistible wiles, but those kinds of non sequitirs bubble up all the time when two people ride together. There's only so much commentary you can make on the rolling countryside before conversation turns to more personal things.

"I guess it depends," I'd said. "On a person's relationship with sex and how bad the breakup was."

She'd laughed. "I was looking for a pat answer."

"You'll never get a pat answer from me about anything. I'm like Socrates. I turn every answer into a question."

Two weeks before the big ride, she'd dropped

this one: "You know what's weird? For the first time in my life, I don't feel the need to be in a couple. At all."

My heart sank. I made a show of carefully inspecting the paper wrapper of my Italian ice for leaks so she wouldn't see the disappointment written all over my face. "Good for you. So no dating for you ever again?"

She tapped her feet against the sidewalk. The metal cleats on her shoes made a crisp *click-click* against the concrete. "That's the funny part. I don't know. I think I could be happy that way. But sometimes when you realize you don't need something—that's the moment when you're ready to have it."

I wanted that kind of confidence, and when I was on the bike, I had it. Getting to the top of a hill or flying down a crest made me feel like I was king of the world.

But whenever my feet left the pedals for solid ground, I returned to my shy and somewhat awkward self, making weird historical references no one understood and liking bad puns more than anyone should. I never knew what to say or do to show my interest in another woman. I'd always been that way, waiting for someone else to make the first move and giving up when they didn't.

The rest of that September day was perfect:

high sixties, a light breeze, and scattered cumulous clouds that made the sun feel refreshing rather than relentless. We got to the shore around 4 p.m., checked our bikes and went straight to the beach house we'd rented with a few other riders. We were sharing a room with two double beds.

"How's your pain doing?" I said as I began unpacking my clothes.

"Much better, thank you. Your seat adjustment worked wonders. My pelvic bone still feels a little bruised, but the fleshy parts are—well, maybe a little tender, but mostly fine." She threw her duffel bag on the bed farthest from the door, pulled out a bathing suit and started stripping her clothes off. "God, it feels good to get out of these disgusting shorts. It'll feel even better to get into that ocean. It's so invigorating this time of year."

I looked away, but not until after catching a glimpse of her ass. It was my first time seeing it, and it was breathtaking.

"You don't have to avoid looking at me." Her voice came over my shoulder. "I don't think I have anything that will shock you. And if I do, it's better you learn now."

"How's that?" I pulled my bra off through the armholes of my cycling jersey.

"You know, in case I want to sleep naked tonight. Or in case we both do."

I looked over my shoulder toward her, but didn't turn all the way. I didn't have to. There was a mirror on the wall, and I could see all of her in it.

Her jersey and bra were off now, leaving only stripes in her skin where the elastic had been. She was still gorgeous. Her breasts drooped slightly under their own weight, their coppery nipples as large as silver dollars.

She met my eyes in the reflection. Was it a challenge? If it was, I wasn't prepared for it.

My throat went dry. "I brought pajamas."

She shrugged. "It's up to you."

We threw sundresses over our bathing suits and bought the largest custard cones known to humankind before finding a spot on the beach. We were starving, and since we would be riding back to Philadelphia the next day, we figured we might as well carbo-load now. My stomach grew full and tiredness started to hit me; when I was done with my cone I lay back and closed my eyes. It felt good, the sun lighting up my eyelids and the sound of the waves in my ears.

When I opened my eyes, the sun was in a different place in the sky and Morgan was leaning over me, whispering, "Wake up, sleepyhead. The last thing you want is a sunburn."

She was so close I could smell the remnants of frozen coffee custard on her tongue. I could smell her sunblock too, and the sheen of sweat she hadn't yet washed off. It reminded me of sex. I wanted to bury myself in it.

"I still have sunblock on," I grumbled, but she was right. If I was going to sleep, it should be back in the beach house.

"Come on." She stood up and grabbed my hand to pull me with her. "The ocean cures everything."

I wasn't so sure about that when, a minute later, I found myself knee-deep in the freezing tide. "Crap, this is cold."

"The perfect thing for tired muscles and a weary groin," Morgan said, lowering herself into the water until only her shoulders and head bobbed above it. Her hair floated around her like seaweed, reminding me of all those drawings of mermaids I used to make when I was a kid and in love with Disney's Ariel, princess of the sea.

Desire flooded me. My calves could barely feel anything thanks to the cold, but the rest of me felt too much. I wanted to kiss Morgan now, under the bright blue sky.

I wanted to do much more than kiss her.

I sank into the water next to her, almost kneeling. The briskness of the water was as shocking as an orgasm. I gasped just as loud.

"I like that sound," Morgan said. She reached for my hand under the water and found it. We linked our fingers. She leaned in closer. "I'd like to hear more where that came from."

"You're an incorrigible flirt today, aren't you?" I said breathlessly.

"For you? Always." She slipped her hand from mine, ran her fingers along my waist and down my hip, stopping at the top of my thigh. The ocean lifted and rocked us, moving like a heartbeat through both our bodies. As it rose, we rose with it, standing tall. As it receded, we sank, our knees descending into the seabed. "Does it bother you?"

I was too cold to blush. "Only if you don't mean anything by it."

"I mean everything by it." And then, her lips close to my ear, as if her words were too private to even share with the ocean, "We've been beating around the bush, haven't we?"

My brain chose that inopportune moment to notify me of the double entendre of *beat* and *bush*. What was I, twelve?

Measured by sense of humor, yes. I started to laugh. Then tried to stop laughing.

Of course, that just resulted in me laughing harder.

She looked at me, bewildered.

I had to explain myself. I didn't want her to think I was laughing *at* her. "It's funny because beating around the bush is the opposite of what we've been doing. Technically speaking."

Well, that was it. Now she'd know for sure how much of a catch I wasn't. I considered ducking under the water and staying there until I reached the shore.

But then I heard her own laughter, louder than seagulls cawing above us. "Well, yeah. If you mean us together. Though, to be honest, I beat around my own bush pretty often."

I didn't think it was possible to get any wetter, submerged in the ocean as I already was. But the image that came into my mind's eye made me flood the lining of my swimsuit. "That's … hot," was all I could think to say.

She smiled. "You know what's even hotter?"

I shook my head.

She leaned in and said in that same private voice from earlier, "Lately, the thing that gets me off the hardest is thinking about you."

My clit stood at attention despite the freezing water. I forgot about how tired I was, about the people on the boardwalk who might see us, about the sand that had washed into the back of my suit and made my skin itch. Morgan and the ocean were all I saw and smelled and heard. I looked the drops of water coalescing on her shoulder, sparkling in the late afternoon sun as if they were giving off their own light.

I kissed one of those drops. It was salty and warm, and Morgan shuddered. "Oh," she said, in soft surprise.

I kissed her mouth next.

Her lips were warm and wind-chapped. She opened them like she was ready to devour me for dinner. She slipped her finger under the opening of my swimsuit.

Up until that moment, I'd forgotten myself along with my tiredness. Maybe that's what had let me be brave enough to kiss her, even though I wasn't on my bike.

But with her finger slipping over my clit, I came back to my body. I was in it, and still unafraid.

I wanted her to devour me.

I moaned something like *yes* into her mouth, or tried to. Our tongues were too tangled for words. She pulled back, just slightly, then pressed her lips to my cheek as she spoke, as if she couldn't bear to separate completely. "I want to taste you."

We ran the whole way. Desire made our bodies forget they'd just ridden eighty miles. We rinsed off together in the enclosed outdoor shower, kissing and clinging as we pulled off our suits and the water poured over us.

"I'm torn between making you come now and waiting until we're inside," she said as she lifted her mouth off my breast.

"Do both." Was that me speaking? Yes. I had become someone else, and I liked it.

She crooked an eyebrow. "Yeah? Can you handle it?"

I spread my legs to give her access to my clit and reached for hers, but she swatted my hand away. "Not yet. Too sore. I'll need something more gentle."

I spoke my deepest desire. "My tongue?"

"Yeah." She pressed her lips to mine, opening her mouth as she stroked two fingers up and down either side of my clit. The water made things tricky, washing most of my lubrication away, but there was still enough that she managed to slide one finger inside me, quickly followed by another. I grunted into her mouth and spread myself wider, propping one foot against the wooden shower wall as my cunt spasmed around her, my breaths shallow and desperate.

She brought her thumb to my clit, swiping it back and forth across the hardened nub. Heat built up in me. I felt like I was going to melt, or explode. I wanted to come and I also fought against it. The sensation was almost too intense, terrifying and wonderful, like hurtling down a steep, winding road on my bicycle, the wind growing louder in my ears as I built up speed, each slight maneuver the only difference between crashing and soaring.

Our kissing grew messy. She ran her free hand over my wet breast, gave it a firm squeeze as she pressed harder against my clit and slid a third finger inside me, moaning as if she was the one being touched.

It was the sound that did me in. I sucked her tongue into my mouth and came, wave after wave crashing over me.

"God, you're hot," she whispered against my neck as I tried to catch my breath. "Even better than I'd imagined."

In our bedroom, Morgan said my cunt tasted

like honey. I said that was flattering, but probably inaccurate from an objective point of view. Her laugh lit up her eyes.

To me, she tasted like the ocean had seeped into her crevices and was now pouring back out. I worked my tongue around her swollen clit until she begged. "Suck it, Lori, please." She squeezed her thighs against my head in her excitement; I pushed them back open to get better access, bringing her hard nub between my lips and drawing my cheeks in. She cried out—her legs quaking, her clit throbbing against my tongue.

"You can—*oh*, um… I… mmm … I came, you can—"

I looked up and smiled at her. "Keep going?"

Her cheeks and chest were flushed pink, her chest heaving. "I was going to stay you can stop, but since you're offering…"

"If it doesn't hurt, I want to keep going."

Her look was perplexed. "Why would it hurt?"

"Your bike saddle?"

"Oh." Her eyes went wide. "Funny, I forgot all about that."

"Good. Let me help you forget some more." I dove back in between her legs.

My pajamas never made it out of my travel bag. We fucked throughout the night and slept less that we should have. Still, when the alarm went off in the morning, I had no regrets.

"How's your crotch?" I couldn't resist asking as we rode off at daybreak. The sun hid behind some low clouds, giving the sky a grayish-pink cast and turning the ocean steel blue as we road along the shore.

"Never been better."

"Never? You exaggerate."

She pursed her mouth as if she were lost in thought. "No. Definitely not exaggerating. I don't think my crotch has ever been so happy." She glanced over at me. "I'm pretty happy too."

We turned a curve in the road so that the ocean was now behind us. "So you're ready for another eighty miles?" I said.

"Of course." She smiled, and just at that moment the sun came out of hiding. Its light shimmered across her skin. She seemed to be glowing from the inside. "With you, I'm ready for anything."

Water & Air

AT THE LAKE WHERE THE water witches
gathered, there lived a girl who didn't know her
own power. I was that girl.

Or *woman*, rather, by the time this particular
summer came. I was fresh out of my first year of
college and back home for the break. I'd grown
into independence in the previous year: living away
from home for the first time, working two jobs to
pay rent and utilities, making my own curfew and
household rules. In all honesty, my rules weren't
much different than my parents'. But they were
mine, and that made all the difference. I was
starting to feel like an adult.

I worked the concession stand at the lake that
summer. The lake was always quiet the first few
weeks of the season—just locals and a few random
tourists who started trickling in around Memorial
Day.

But then the witches would descend. They'd begin arriving a week or so before the summer solstice and kept coming in droves until the fall equinox.

I never really understood the attraction of our lake to the water witches. Anywhere they were, they could draw water vapor from the air and force it to condense—so why they needed a lake to hang out in was beyond me. I'd heard something about the lake being sacred, or a source for rejuvenating their powers, but I wasn't sure how accurate any of that was. They mostly seemed to be there to have fun.

Swimming at the lake as a young girl, I'd watch them with fascination as they formed bright, clear spheres of water from seemingly nothing, then pop them over each other's heads like water balloons. Shrieks and giggles always followed, and then a game of one-upmanship with miniature waterfalls appearing out of thin air, elaborate fountains suddenly springing up in the middle of the lake and—the locals' least favorite trick—the occasional impromptu thunderstorm.

The double and triple rainbows that came afterward usually made the inconvenience of unpredicted rain worth it to me. Not that I ever would have admitted that to a water witch.

Like most of the locals, I had a love-hate relationship with the water witches. They made our summers more interesting, and kept our town's economy from tanking into a permanent depression.

But they weren't *us*.

And I'd spent most of my childhood bewildered by their levity.

My grandmother had been a fire witch, but she didn't use her gift to goof off. She was constantly making emergency trips out west to Colorado and California to help manage the wildfires there.

In high school, I finally asked her what she thought of the water witches' constant partying.

"That's only the part you see," she said. "So you think they don't care about anything serious. But that's how *everyone* is when they're on vacation. The rest of the time, they slog through like the rest of us." She pulled out a box of photos from her trips out west she'd never gotten around to organizing. She showed me a group shot of about 40 people— half were ungifted firefighters, the other half witches. I'd seen the photo before, and had always assumed all the witches in it were fire witches.

"Of course not," she said to me, rolling her eyes. "Sandra over here was a water witch, and Janie and Becca and these two whose names I don't remember. They helped make the fire breaks. Stacy and Jenna over here were earth witches. They smothered fires with dirt, and sped up the decomposition of kindling so it wouldn't catch— that sort of thing. And we even had an air witch. Now that's powerful magic. She could still the winds to keep the fire from spreading. She could even do stuff with electricity and remove oxygen from air, but we never used those gifts much."

I wanted to be like my grandmother. From my earliest childhood, I would focus my energy on sunbeams and try to will them into sparks of flame. When it was time to snuff out the candles at winter solstice, I'd just stare at them, hoping I could extinguish them with my thoughts alone.

"Staring won't put a fire out," my mom would tease. She knew exactly what I was doing, because she'd done the same as a girl.

"Believe me, Miranda, I've tried. But we can't all be witches. Your grandmother is the only one we've had in this family in generations. Magic is a crapshoot that way."

I finally accepted my mother's admonitions and turned my energies to studying instead. If I couldn't engage with the natural world by magical means, I would do it the old-fashioned way: science.

Everything I took outside of freshman comp my first year at college fell within the sciences. Chemistry turned out to be my favorite. I became obsessed with it. It could do many of the things that magic could, but without requiring the chemist to have any special gift.

I decided to get ready for the organic chemistry course I'd be taking in fall of my sophomore year by reading the textbook over the summer. It's what I was reading behind the concession stand when the first water witch of the summer strolled in.

She was an attractive young woman about my age, with an appealing smile and long natural hair that radiated from her head in tight black curls. "I could just die for a blue raspberry slushie right now," she said when I asked for her order. "Extra-large. It's so freaking hot out today."

"You could make it rain," I said.

"I wish. But I'm not that powerful. Besides, you know how the locals would feel about that." She winked at me. I wondered if she was flirting. I went to grab a cup from next to the slushie machine and immediately dropped it. My face flushed red. I turned my back to her and grabbed another cup, successfully getting it under the dispenser this time.

I willed my cheeks to cool down as the cup filled. I wasn't a blushing virgin, and I didn't want her to think I was one. Not that it should matter what she thought. She was just another water witch out for a self-indulgent summer on the lake, with no interest in the townsfolk. The fact that she was smoking hot was irrelevant.

Fortunately, a breeze blew through the stand, just cool enough to dissipate the heat from my cheeks. I turned around and gave her the slushie. "Three-fifty," I said.

She got out her cash and handed it to me. "I've never met an air witch before," she said. "Not a lot of those around."

Well if *that* wasn't the non sequitur of the year. "Me neither," I said. I handed her the change.

She frowned. "That must be hard for you. How

do you learn to develop your magic?"

I stared at her. "Sorry, I'm not following?"

"You just did that thing with the wind. You're an air witch, right?"

"The wind?" I said incredulously. "The wind is a natural phenomenon caused by changes in air pressure. I had nothing to do with it."

She looked down at her hands, busying herself by putting her wallet back in her purse. "Sorry," she said quietly. "My mistake. I just got this vibe from you. I could have sworn you were a witch.

Not that you can tell by looking at a person, it's just...."

I felt bad for her. She was cute and sweet, and even if she was an outsider—well, that wasn't her fault. Besides, I had a soft spot for attractive ladies. "I think your witchdar and your gaydar crossed wires," I said. "I'm queer. But no magix."

She burst out laughing. "Oh, silly me. My first day ever at the lake and I would make a mistake like that." She hung her purse back over her shoulder and smiled at me coyly. "Sometimes when I find myself talking to a lovely lady, I get all confuddled."

I blushed again, but this time I didn't mind if she saw. Which was good, because no breeze came to my rescue. "I'm Miranda Peterson." I reached out my hand. "Nice to meet you."

She shook it. Her skin was as smooth as a plum. "Hazel Green," she said. "*Enchantée*."

We started hanging out, Hazel and me. We'd walk around in the shade of the forest on the lake's edge, or just spend time out on the beach, watching the other witches playing in the water. Sometimes we would swim. Those were always my favorite afternoons, because her skin shimmered like dark chocolate ganache when she came up out of the water, and her nipples made tight little peaks against the fabric of her bikini when she got cold.

She didn't do much magic around me at first. She was self-conscious about it, having been a late bloomer who only discovered her gift a few years earlier, her junior year of high school.

This was her first time at a gathering, and she had so much practice to do before she could accomplish anything that really mattered, she said. "I'm not like the water witches your grandmother worked with," she said, and I immediately regretted telling her about Grandma's adventures out west. "The things I can do feel frivolous in comparison to what I want to achieve."

I squeezed her hand. "We all feel like that sometimes. That's how it is in chemistry lab when I'm trying to separate hydrogen peroxide into water and air. It's been done before, and it doesn't really help anyone. But we all have to learn the basic steps before we can really dance."

The next day I brought my organic chemistry textbook with me to the beach. I plunked it down between us on the blanket. "If I can do chemistry in front of you," I said, "you can do magic in front of me."

It helped her loosen up. As the days unfolded, she'd practice making bubbles and balloons and tiny little rain clouds that would hover inches above my head and break open when I complained too much about the heat.

"No you don't!" I squealed the dozenth time she attacked me with one of those rain clouds. "Not unless you get wet, too!" I pulled her close to me as the cloud burst over our heads.

"You devil!" she said with absolutely no malice. Her eyes were level with mine, her amused lips not even inches away. Her breasts were pressed against mine, and I could feel the breath move in and out of her, each a little faster than the one that came before.

I kissed her then for the first time. The rain stopped, evaporating into a double rainbow.

We made love soon after. It had been too long in the waiting. I'd been spending a lot of time watching her move in her body: the way she tilted her hips just so when she crossed her legs, and how when she uncrossed them, her bikini hem would reveal the tiniest hint of pubic hair at the crux of her mons and thigh.

I had watched her move in her body, and now I wanted to move in it, too.

And yet— "Are you sure you want to do this?" I

said as she reached her hand into the front of my bikini bottoms, teasing her fingers along my pubic bone. We were on the beach at night. It was quieter then, with most of the witches having retreated into the woods for moonlight rituals. Hazel had created a curtain of rain around us to give us privacy from the few people who remained on the beach.

"It's okay if I don't go to the rituals every night, if that's what you mean." She kissed up my shoulder to my neck. "I learn a lot there, but it's good to take a break every now and then. Especially if it's with you."

"That's not what I mean," I said, though it was hard to get the words out with her body moving against mine. "I mean I'm not magic. I can't do what you can." I'd heard vague stories of what witches could do in bed. The magic was part of their bodies. Using it to fuck would be as natural to her as licking or fingering would be to me. Compared to every tool she had at her disposal, my repertoire seemed rather limited.

She nibbled at my ear. "I've been wanting to make you wet in a way that has nothing to do with water witchcraft ever since I met you. Haven't you wanted that too?"

I nodded my head and dropped my thighs open. "So much."

"Good." She reached down farther, sliding her finger into my wet vulva. "Because you make me so hot. I don't care if you can't do magic. I want your body on me."

"But I wish I could—" I started. My breath hitched as she pushed her finger inside me—though *pushed* hardly seemed the right word. I was so hungry for her, it might be more accurate to say I was the one who was moving: taking her in, enveloping her, swallowing her whole.

"Can you use your hands?" she whispered, curling her finger and brushing it against the front wall of my vagina.

My eyes rolled back in my head. "Yes."

"And your mouth?" She bent down and tugged at my bikini bra with her teeth, exposing my nipple to the warm night air. She took it in her mouth, sucking on it lavishly.

"God yes," I said.

"Good." She kissed up my throat to my lips. "You use what powers you have to get me off, and I'll use mine on you."

I didn't argue with her anymore. I pulled off her bikini top and kissed her breasts—small, pert little mounds, each just the right size to fit in my mouth. She lay down under me, letting her thighs fall open against the beach blanket, and I worked down her body.

"Take these off." I tugged at her bikini bottoms as my mouth reached her navel.

She looked down at me. "You take them off. And then eat me. I want you to taste how wet you make me."

That was all I needed. I tugged at the strings that tied the bikini in place over her hips. The skimpy piece of fabric fell open, revealing her glorious thatch of dark pubic hair. I combed my fingers through it, pushing it back to reveal the seam between her fleshy mons. I pressed my tongue in, licking up the soft ridges of her vulva, smooth strokes from her vagina to her clit and back.

"Oh Miranda," she gasped. "That's all the magic I need."

I pressed in closer, my lips and tongue dragging over her in tandem. Her taste was slightly sweet, reminiscent of honey and persimmons. This was the drink I'd been craving for weeks.

She moaned and pushed her crotch into my face as I worked her over, a pleasingly steady pressure of flesh against flesh as she oozed wetness into my mouth and down my chin. I went from long, flat-tongued licks to hard, probing ones, pushing past her vulva and into her sweet, throbbing cunt.

"Oh yeah, Miranda. Like that."

The curtain of rain that surrounded us began to pound down harder, steady drumming that matched the volume of her cries. I growled into her cunt, sending vibrations deep into her body. She arched her back off the ground, began to beg, "Yes, Miranda, more."

She was soaking now, not from her magic but from me. Her juice mixed with my saliva as it dripped down between her thighs and into the humid furrow of her ass. I followed the trail with one finger, slid it around in her lubrication before teasing it over her clenching asshole.

"This okay?" I said.

She nodded, pulling her knees up to her shoulders to give me better access. "Yeah," she murmured. "I like that. Give it to me in both ends."

I pressed my finger more firmly and her asshole winked, sucking my finger in. Inside was all slick tight heat, her muscle squeezing with every lick I made into her swelling cunt. The rain around us turned into a downpour.

I wanted to eat her out for hours. My own crotch was soaking, my clit throbbing, but I didn't care. I was getting off on her taste and the way she moved and moaned, the way she responded to my ungifted touch.

And then I felt it. A soft lick at first, tentative and experimental between my legs. And then, more firmly, a warm wet pulse against my mons. I parted my legs. The pressure increased and the touch widened, washing down from my ass to my clit. I pulled my knees under my body to expose more of my erogenous zone to the unexpected touch. As it surged against me, I realized what it was: water, summoned by Hazel out of the elements as an extension of her body. She was giving me what I was giving her.

The water kept changing forms as it moved against me. Sometimes it was structured and exploring like a tongue. Other times it spurted against me in quick, steady bursts like water from a showerhead, relentlessly bringing me further toward climax. It wiggled soft and exploring up my cleft, caressed the mounds of my ass and the sensitive dip above my tailbone. It took the shape of hands—not just a pair, but an army of them, massaging my breasts and my anus, tickling the soft skin at the back of my knees, exploring the contours of shoulder blade and thigh. It kissed me, too, with as much passion as her lips would have. It licked me wet and open—probing, prodding, urging me to spread my legs wider and to take more as it slipped into my cunt—a smooth shape that was both liquid and solid, stroking the walls of my vagina like a thousand tiny tongues, expanding and stretching me as far as I could open, sliding up the length of me to tickle my swollen cervix.

My whole body shook. I was being fucked by Hazel outside and in, and all the while never having to separate my tongue from her hot, honeyed pussy.

"I'm gonna come, Miranda, you have no idea, I'm gonna—"

Oh, I had an idea all right. I was right there with her. Electricity throbbed through my body. Wind gusted over us, up to her breasts and face, kissing her everywhere I couldn't kiss her with my mouth. The water responded, fucking deeply into me, laving my vulva and clit and anus. I came like a hurricane, wailing pleasure into the engorged flesh of her cunt, and she came, too, spurting hot and creamy over my hungry tongue.

The wind started to die down. The curtain of rain that surrounded us slowed into a steady pitter-patter.

"What was that?" Hazel whispered as her breathing started to slow.

I pulled myself up to her, kissed her with her honey still on my tongue. She moaned a soft delight. "You just fucked me with water," I whispered against her mouth. "So stop saying your magic isn't powerful."

"Well, I was rather pleased with my performance, if I do say so myself." She batted her eyes. "But that's not what I meant."

"No?" I said. "What were you asking about, then? My finger up your ass?" I smiled coyly. "Was that a first for you?"

"Yes, it was. And it was mind-blowing." Her grin made her teeth shine white in the moonlight. "But that's not what I was asking about either. I meant the wind. If you're not an air witch, where did it come from?"

"It was just—" I started to make the same comment I'd made the first time I met her, when I'd brushed off the breeze as an act of nature. But I suddenly realized I couldn't use that logic tonight.

We were inside an enchanted curtain of rain. Natural breezes couldn't occur here. Natural wind doesn't caress your girlfriend's tits at your beck and call.

And more than that, I had felt her skin where the wind had touched it. Felt her body just as surely as if it had been my fingers on her skin.

The wind and I had been the same thing at that moment.

I was an air witch.

She pulled me close to her. "It's okay that you didn't know," she murmured. "Sometimes this is how gifts are discovered, with us late-bloomers."

"Is that what happened to you?"

She nodded. "I was masturbating in the bath tub. It wasn't the first time I'd masturbated, and I'd had really good orgasms before—so that wasn't what gave birth to the magic. I think what happened was, my body was ready to channel magic, but my mind didn't know how to acknowledge it. Because by the time someone's the age I was, or the age you are—no one expects to become a witch at that age." Hazel sighed. "The magic couldn't come to me until I turned off that preconception. Turned off my mind. And you know how it is when you're touching yourself. My mind turned off. All I could hear was my body. And I followed its call. I let the magic move through me. And when I gave myself over to it, let the water move in the way that felt right... well, I knew. I was a water witch."

I was quiet for a long time, mulling over what she'd told me.

"It's weird," I said. "I spent so much time wanting to be a fire witch like my grandmother, it never occurred to me I might have another kind of magic in my genes."

"Does it bother you, being something you didn't expect?"

I shook my head. "As long as I don't have to stop studying chemistry, I think I'm okay with it."

Hazel laughed—a boisterous, joyful sound that made me feel like I was floating. The breeze picked up and caressed her thighs.

"I don't think you should give up on science. It's always good to have more than one tool in your arsenal."

"Like using both my fingers and tongue to get you off?"

"Exactly. Which reminds me." She rolled me on my back and kissed down my torso and belly, then looked up as she pried my thighs apart. "It would be a shame if you thought the only tool in my arsenal was water. How about I show you what I can do with my tongue?"

She licked me, and the wind blew.

Making Snow

"I'M DISAPPOINTED IN your marketing efforts, Jolie." Steve Pratt set the previous week's numbers report on Jolie's desk. "These figures are pitiful. Your campaigns are ineffective."

Jolie glanced over the report. Average daily visitors to the Pratt Hill Ski Resort had hit an abysmal low of thirteen—mostly early-morning birdwatchers and hikers who enjoyed the challenge of a steep climb. She looked at her stepfather. "It would help if we had snow on the slopes. Maybe you could talk to Chaz about that."

Chaz was Jolie's stepbrother and in charge of maintenance at the resort, and while he couldn't control the fact that there'd been no natural snowfall yet this winter, he should have been able to supply the slopes with artificial powder. But after years of shoddy care, the snow machine system had given up the ghost at the end of the previous season, and Chaz had failed to order replacements, despite having access to a multimillion-dollar emergency equipment fund. Jolie suspected embezzlement—Chaz had been living beyond his means for years, with expensive sports cars and frequent trips to Vegas—but when she'd tried to bring it up with her stepfather, the accusation fell on deaf ears. Chaz was Steve's golden boy.

"Don't put the blame on Chaz. You're the operations manager."

"If I'm the manager, don't you think it's about time you gave me oversight of Chaz's accounts? Or to let me override his purchasing power and order the new equipment myself?"

"What do you know about making snow?"

"I used to be on the snowmaking crew, Dad." Jolie preferred not to use the familiarity with her stepfather, but she hoped it might soften him up.

It failed. "Chaz gets a lot of self-worth from his job. I won't let you take that away from him."

"If we're not going to have snow, we should think about expanding our off-season offerings. Improve the nature trails and market them to—"

"This is a resort, not a national park. If these numbers aren't up soon, you'll be out of a job. We'll all be. Excuses don't fix the problem." He marched off.

Jolie had, in fact, been looking for another job, but with a failing ski resort as the only employer on her resume, interviews were hard to come by. She'd worked here since she was a teenager, moving up the ranks from ski instructor to facilities crew to shift manager to guest services coordinator. When the previous operations manager quit in a huff over the lack of transparency of Chaz's spending, she became the replacement.

She'd once been proud to be part of this operation. Skiing was her one true joy. She'd started on the bunny hill at age four and done her first ski jump on her sixth birthday. It was the only thing that made her feel truly free.

Or would have, if there had been any powder on the hills.

Jolie picked up her cell phone and texted Chaz. *Any word on when we'll have snow?*

No answer came.

It was five o'clock and already dark outside. The sky was frustratingly clear—no purple clouds to reflect the ski-slope lights back to earth. No sign of impending snow at all.

Chaz hadn't shown up to the office at all that day and he hadn't answered her texts. She hadn't seen or heard from him since the previous Thursday, when he'd announced he would be taking a long weekend to "recover from the stress of dealing with the snow machines." Today was Wednesday. Long weekend, indeed. He was probably in Vegas squandering the snow machine money on gambling and hookers. It grated Jolie that her stepbrother was getting more sex than she was. Not that she wanted to hire a hooker, necessarily; she tended toward relationships more than one-night stands, though even the latter were growing harder to come by with the dwindling visitor count to Pratt Hill.

Jolie walked down toward employee housing, flashlight in one hand and keychain in the other. The frigid air felt good in her lungs. She was taking a shortcut created over the years by countless employee footsteps treading up and down the side of the mountain. A nature walk, even in the dark, might help take her mind off Chaz and the resort's business troubles. With the full moon out, it wasn't difficult to see the trail.

The keys in her gloved hand clinked together with each step. She imagined it as the song of the stars that now stood out clearly against the cold sky. Orion, the Big Dipper, and—she craned her head backward—the Milky Way. As long as she'd lived up here, she'd never gotten over how strange the last one looked, a gauzy arc glowing across the sky. At a younger age, she'd thought the Milky Way was where snow was made before it descended into the clouds.

Unconsciously, she tossed her keys lightly into the air and caught them in her hand—throw-catch, throw-catch—increasing the force of her throw with each step.

As she passed the pond, she threw them too hard and failed to catch them. She heard them plunk to the left of the trail and skitter down the short slope before making a sharp clank against the pond ice and skidding out on its surface. *Fuck*. That keychain had everything on it—the keys for her apartment, the office, both lodges' private areas, and the front gate. Steve would blow his top if she asked for replacements.

Jolie shimmied down the incline until she was at the pond's shore, scanning the flashlight's beam across the surface and finding the keys a body's length from shore. Good. She wouldn't have to crawl out far to get them. Hell, she wouldn't have to crawl at all. Here along the edges, the ice would be thick enough to hold her weight.

She shuffled out, first one foot and then another, and had just picked up the keys and tucked them in her pocket when—

Crack. The sound ripped through the night, shaking the stars. Or, wait—the stars weren't the ones moving. It was Jolie—her feet slipping out, her head descending toward the ice, the world whirling as she tried to regain her balance.

There was nothing to balance on.

She plunged into the water. Coldness clawed through her clothing. Her legs were on fire, then her hips, then her heart. Icy water licked into her mouth and ears. She closed her eyes and tried to close her nostrils.

Float. Float. That was the word she kept repeating to herself as she bumped against the undersurface of the ice.

She passed out.

The first thing Jolie noticed when she regained consciousness was that the substance entering her lungs was air, not water. It was warm and light, smelling of sun and hyacinths.

The second thing she noticed was that she was on a solid surface. It curved against her weight, supporting her spine and the muscles of her legs.

She blinked her eyes open. At the center of her vision was a clear, sunny sky. Around the edges, long fingers of grass reached up toward the blue, their seed heads quavering in the breeze as she stirred.

She sat up to find herself in a meadow in full bloom. Pink rue and purple lupine, red poppies and yellow coreopsis, blue delphiniums and green Irish bells jostled in the wind. She couldn't remember ever seeing a field so filled with flowers. Didn't delphiniums and poppies usually bloom at different times of year?

Stranger still were the small flecks of white that came floating through the air toward her.

Snow.

She rubbed her eyes. Surely she must be seeing things. But when she refocused them the flecks looked just the same. And now there were more. They moved toward her, a silently swarming cloud.

The first flake to touch her felt like a kiss—cool

at first, then warming as it thawed against her skin. There was another, then another—one to her brow, one to her ear, one to her neck, each more sensual than the previous one, dissolving into a heat that felt like desire. The kisses climbed up her calves and descended her arms. She realized she was no longer in her winter clothes. Her coat was gone, her feet bare. She wore a sleeveless linen shift that came down to her thighs. Underneath—

She lifted the hem of her dress and found herself naked. A breeze tickled her pubic hair and the grass. She spread her legs. Snow drifted into the crevice, landing on her mons.

She shivered, but not from the cold. The snowflake felt like a lover's lips, firm and self-assured. She sank back into the grass and spread herself wider. More snowflakes—impossibly warm—kissed her. They became a blizzard, melting against her sex, tonguing at her, opening her. She was being indulged by a dozen lovers. She spread herself open with the fingers of one hand, then pushed two from the other into her wetness. They slid in easily. She groaned.

"Aren't you beautiful?"

Jolie looked up with a start. A tall, ageless woman stood just a few feet away. She was pale, with sun-bleached hair as white as the snow that filled the air and a linen dress longer than Jolie's. The woman's skirt blew in the same direction as the snow. She smiled and her teeth were as bright as stars.

She was the most beautiful creature Jolie had ever seen.

Jolie slid her fingers from her body and wiped them through the grass, cleaning them with the snow crystals that had accumulated there. She tugged down her skirt. "I'm sorry. I didn't know there was anyone around."

"It's alright. I didn't mean to startle you. Carry on." She spoke without a hint of irony, as if there was nothing salacious about walking upon an almost-thirty-year-old woman masturbating in the snow.

"No, that's …" The blizzard was tapering off into a light flurry. "That's all right. It's something I usually do alone."

The woman cocked her head. Snowflakes clung to her hair in a bright crown. "Never with someone else?"

Jolie felt her face flush. "That too. It's been a while, though."

"You're fetching. I'm sure you'll have no trouble finding partners around here, if you wish. You're a traveler, I assume? I've never seen you before."

Jolie thought about the question. Was she a traveler? She didn't remember traveling here. But she knew this wasn't her home, either. So she nodded. "Yes."

"My name is Kindra." The woman offered her hand. Jolie looked down at her own, which still smelled of her juices even if they no longer glistened with them.

"Um ..."

"Your fragrance is appealing. I wouldn't mind having some of it on my skin."

Jolie's face burned hotter, but she accepted the offered hand and allowed Kindra to tug her to her feet. The tug was quick, pulling Jolie close to her face. Kindra's plump pink lips were at the level of Jolie's eyes. "I'm Jolie."

"Nice to meet you, Jolie. Where are you staying?"

"I ... I don't know. I'm not sure how I got here."

"You're welcome to stay with me until your memory returns. I don't bite."

Disappointment clutched Jolie's chest. She found herself wishing that Kindra *did* bite. Her teeth were so large and pretty, and to feel them pressing lightly against her nipples or harder against her shoulder or ass would be a delight. "I would love to. Stay with you, that is. If it's not a bother."

The air was once again clear and blue. Only a few bright flakes remained on the grass and Kindra's hair as evidence that it had snowed. "No bother at all."

They slept in separate rooms. This was a disappointment to Jolie, but she didn't say so. Besides, her quarters were extravagantly comfortable, with a feather bed and down-filled duvet and pillows. She felt like she was sleeping inside a cloud.

After breakfast the next morning, Kindra came into Jolie's room to fluff the bedding out. She whipped the duvet into the air and snapped it vigorously. Tiny white plumes emerged from the ticking, rising up like unsettled dust—first one, and then another, until soon the room was filled with a storm of delicate feathers as thick as the previous day's blizzard. They tickled Jolie's skin as they floated past her toward the window, each a finger that left a trail of desire in its wake. As they emerged into the full sun of outdoors, she noticed a change: each feathery plume transformed into a snowflake.

Jolie gasped and spun around. She could barely make out Kindra's pale skin or white dress among the countless feathers filling the air. "But how—?" As Jolie spoke the words, a plume settled into her mouth and dissolved into water.

"I am the mother of snow." Kindra's voice rose through the feathers' flutter. "When I shake the bedding, it brings snow to your world."

"But we haven't had snow in ages." Jolie knew this much even if she couldn't remember anything else about the place she'd come from.

"It's difficult to keep up with the world's demands. The Atlantic seaboard, the Rockies, the Andes, Mongolia, the Pyrenees, Kilimanjaro … I can never make enough for them all. If one has enough, another falls short."

"I'll help, then." Jolie made her way toward the bed and picked up a pillow. She tossed it into the air until her arms were weak and trembling. Then she started with the next pillow. How long they went on, she couldn't tell. She was breathless and wobbly muscled when the last loose feather drifted out the window.

Despite the infinite number of feathers that had escaped the ticking, the bedding was even loftier than it had been the night before. Jolie collapsed onto it. She felt like she was floating. "That was exhausting."

Kindra settled beside her. "I can't disagree. It works even better with two. Perhaps your home will get snow now."

"It still wouldn't be enough," Jolie sighed. "We're so behind."

"I'll beat my bed again in a bit, then."

"You don't have to."

Kindra squeezed her hand. "It's my pleasure."

Jolie drifted off to sleep.

Jolie awoke to soft moans. She sat up. Kindra was no longer by her side.

Another moan—or perhaps it would be better described as a whimper, though whether of pain, pleasure, frustration, or exertion, Jolie couldn't tell. She cocked her head to locate the sound's source, and as she did so a movement outdoors caught her eye. She stepped toward the window and peered out to find snow again streaming from the house and out over the meadow. This time it came from Kindra's window instead of her own.

Another moan, louder this time. It was obviously a moan of exertion, if the flurry of flakes emerging from Kindra's room was anything to go by. She must be shaking the bedding with every bit of her strength. Still, the moan's low octave reverberated through Jolie's pelvis, made her sex tingle with want. She rubbed herself lightly through her dress.

You can touch yourself later, you perv, she scolded herself. *Go and help.*

Kindra's door was open, and Kindra was indeed exerting herself—but not in the way Jolie had expected. Kindra was naked, knees planted on the featherbed, legs splayed, one hand at the juncture of her thighs, pumping furiously. Two fingers in her cunt and her thumb in her ass, sliding in, out, in, out, Kindra writhing and panting against the pillows, rubbing her breasts against the duvet, her free hand curled around the bed rail, gripping tight with pleasure.

Feathers swirled around Kindra's naked body.

Kindra let out another sound—a slow, crescendoing wail that rattled Jolie's ribcage and shook more feathers free from the ticking. Jolie stepped closer, not wanting the feathers to obscure her view. They fell against her skin, soft as hair or tongues or, perhaps, the smooth translucent fur that bordered Kindra's pink cunt.

Jolie could smell it now, as rich and heavy as honey. She let out her own moan.

Kindra looked over her shoulder, but didn't seem startled. She kept working her fingers into her body. Her pale gray eyes bore into Jolie's heart. "You've come. I'm glad. I wanted to show you the other way to shake the bedding." And with that she turned away again, craned her neck down to take her own breast into her mouth, and came so hard the floor quaked.

The air went white, as blank and invariable as a piece of copy paper. Feathers surrounded Jolie, billowing against her, molding against her body the way her bed had just a few moments before. She closed her eyes and sank into them—floating, falling, until she found herself on the bed next to Kindra, the last of the feathers floating away.

"That's quite a way to shake out the bed," Jolie said.

"It works even better with two."

Jolie became acutely aware of her own sweet, sticky syrup clinging to the inside of her thighs. She looked into Kindra's eyes and grew wetter. "I could help."

"I wouldn't want to wear you out."

"I don't mind. We need snow at home and you need help making it. Sounds like a win-win to me."

"Well, when you put it that way—" Kindra chuckled and leaned in for a kiss.

Kindra's lips were warmer than feathers or snow

but had the same sort of melting quality, making Jolie's mouth and cunt go slick and her skin bloom with sweat. Kindra slipped her tongue past the seam of Jolie's lips; Jolie moaned as if it had sunk between her legs. Soon Kindra's wet fingers *were* between Jolie's legs, smoothing over Jolie's mons and teasing down the rift.

Jolie spread herself wide. She couldn't remember ever feeling so wanton, even yesterday in the grassy meadow with a thousand snowflakes teasing her skin and the air redolent with the scent of hyacinths.

"So lovely," Kindra murmured. She tugged Jolie's dress off and kissed down her body with a measured slowness, as if she was exploring a new landscape and didn't want to miss any of its features. Jolie shuddered and whined, arching off the bed with each unexpected touch. Feathers lifted into the air, first as lone puffs, then in large clouds as desire moved more forcefully through Jolie's heart and hips. Everywhere Kindra kissed—Jolie's collarbone, her breasts, her belly, her clit—felt like it was thawing.

"I want—" Jolie muttered, and then again, "I want—" But she found she couldn't finish the sentence because she didn't know exactly what she wanted. She wanted to come and she wanted this to last forever. She wanted Jolie's mouth on her breasts and her cunt. She wanted—

"How about this?" Kindra flipped Jolie over onto her knees: her ass in the air, her cunt exposed.

Feathers whirled around them, fluttered across Jolie's back and breasts. She arched forward and back, seeking more of their touch.

"Don't you worry, darling. There will be plenty of feathers soon." Kindra sank her mouth onto Jolie's ripe cunt, licking her lips and clit. Jolie was soaring up a hill, or maybe barreling down one, the wind strong against her face, the adrenalin pounding in her veins as snow went flying.

Kindra worked her tongue into Jolie's cunt, then her fingers as she licked up to the sensitive skin of Jolie's ass. Jolie arced with shock and pleasure, freeing another cloud of feathers from the bedding.

"You like that?" Kindra purred.

Jolie could only nod and grip at the duvet as Kindra sank back in.

Jolie felt the way she did every time she flew off a ski jump: powerful, terrified, and on a knife's sharp edge between life and death, control and surrender. It was ecstasy.

She came with the force of an avalanche.

"I remembered who I am," Jolie said as the last feathers drifted out the window like so many dandelion seeds.

"And where you're from?" Kindra ran her fingers absentmindedly over Jolie's belly.

Jolie could see the side of the mountain at night, snowless and with a clear sky. She saw Orion over her head and the spun-sugar diaphany of the Milky Way. She shook her head to scatter the vision away. She wasn't ready to return. "I'm getting there. But I'd like to stay here a little longer, if that's alright with you."

"It's my pleasure to have you here."

Jolie smirked. "Is it? Would you like to have me again?"

Kindra didn't miss a beat. She slid her hands up Jolie's arms and pinned her wrists against the pillows. "We'll have each other." She climbed up the bed and swung her legs over Jolie's shoulder, sinking her spread cunt onto Jolie's mouth. She tasted as good as she smelled, like nectar and fresh snow.

They fucked for days. Weeks. Feathers filled the house. Snowflakes blanketed the meadow in white. When they got up to eat or drink or bathe, Jolie would gaze out the window, watching as the snow evaporated to reveal the life beneath. The grass and flowers only seemed to grow stronger, their colors richer with each passing storm.

Jolie's memories surfaced along with her orgasms. One detail, then another. She knew who she was, where she was from, and why she didn't want to go back. Yet at the same time, she also knew that the slopes called to her.

"It's time," she said one evening as moon sliced

its blade of light through the haze of feathers and snow filling Kindra's bedroom. Their bedroom. Jolie had never returned to the guest room since that first night.

"All right. I'll show you how to get there." Kindra slipped out of bed and slid her dress on over her head. She was a snow-capped peak. She offered Jolie her hand.

They walked through the meadow to the place where Kindra had found Jolie that first day. Jolie was surprised to see two trees on either side of it, framing the spot like a doorway. Beyond it she saw an icy pond, its smooth surface interrupted by a jagged aperture near its shore. Water lapped against the frozen edges as if something had just splashed through it.

Wind gusted over the pond and between the trees. For the first time since arriving in this place, Jolie felt real coldness. She stared at the ice and shivered. "Maybe not yet."

"No? But you're ready."

"First—" Jolie pressed Kindra up against the tree and kissed her. "Just once, I want to fuck you without making snow. I want to fuck you for no other reason than wanting you."

Kindra melted against her. She let her dress fall to the ground. Jolie pulled her down into the grass. They feasted on each other until they were hoarse from moaning. Jolie climaxed so hard she saw snow.

Snow. It fell all around as Jolie broke through the pond's surface, gasping for air. She threw her arms onto the ice and pressed on it, testing its ability to take her weight before lifting herself flat-bellied onto its surface. She crawled onto shore.

Jolie was usually the first person to arrive at the office, but when she showed up the next morning, her stepfather was already standing over her desk, a scowl on his face despite the thick blanket of snow outside.

She checked her watch. She was on time, but saying so wouldn't appease him. Mentioning that she'd almost drowned, been transported to another dimension, taken on a new lover with mind-blowing sexual prowess, awoke in a freezing pond, and then spent the bulk of the evening making sure she didn't have hypothermia probably wouldn't save her, either. She bit her tongue.

"Good morning, Steve. What's up?"

"Nothing good, I'm afraid."

She put on a happy face. "There's a foot of snow on the slopes. And they're predicting more each night this week. Business should pick up."

"Yes, that's good, but—" Steve gestured to a piece of paper on her desk. "I found that last night when I got home. From Chaz."

Jolie's eyes flicked over the paper:

Dear Dad,

When you receive this letter, I will no longer be in the country.

For the past several years I've been using the emergency fund as my own personal credit card. That habit caught up with me this year.

I wasted a lot of the money in ways that can never be recovered. But some of it might be. Attached is a list of assets I've signed over to you: stocks, properties, jewelry, bank accounts, etc. I hope it's enough to keep the resort afloat and give you a chance to recover.

Sincerely, Chaz

Steve sniffled. "The police have been trying to track him down, but no luck so far. You were right. I was wrong."

"I'm not sure that matters. We're still both fucked."

He sank down in a chair. Looked up at her. He was a dog with his tail between his legs. "I would deserve that, but you don't. I've been up all night talking with lawyers and financial advisors. Apparently the stocks have shot up in value since he signed them over. And some of the properties are worth a lot more than he thought. We won't be able to recoup everything, but with a little credit and the money that comes in from liquidating those assets, we should be able to get a working snow system this season. A savvy operating manager once told me a lack of snow was the main thing holding this place back, so ... when all this is over, she should probably get a raise."

"We'll cross that bridge when we come to it. In the meantime I should probably start calling manufacturers."

"Yes. And I'll deal with the money. But this time—" Steve cleared his throat. "I'll keep you in the loop about the finances."

Jolie watched her stepfather walk out of her office and close the door behind him. She wished she could gloat, but she only felt tired.

She looked out the window and watched the snow fall. Through it, she imagined she could see Kindra, naked and arching on her feather bed.

Natural snowfall fell at record levels that winter, keeping the slopes covered until the new snow system was operational. Visitors came and so did money. The resort began to recover And Jolie got her raise and a bigger office. She no longer wanted to leave Pratt Hill. Chaz was arrested in Thailand.

It was summer now. From her office window, Jolie watched a group of hikers gather in the parking lot as she waited for the next interviewee to arrive. The resort had grown more popular in the off-season since announcing its long-term trail and native-flower improvement plan—one of the many things the new facilities manager would oversee along with snowmaking in the winter.

Jolie heard a throat clear behind her. It was her office assistant. "Your next interview has arrived. Résumé's in here." He dropped a folder on her desk.

"Thanks, bring them in." Jolie opened the folder. A committee had vetted the applications and chosen the final candidates, and this was Jolie's first time reading this résumé. She gasped when she saw the name at the top.

"I'm sorry. Is now a bad time?"

Jolie looked up to find a tall woman with pale skin and hair bleached white by the sun. Recognition danced in her gray eyes.

"Kindra? You're Kindra Snow?"

Kindra nodded. "Yes. I'm applying for the facilities position. I specialize in snow manufacture and grooming, but I also have experience with native landscaping. And ... you look strangely familiar. Have we met before?"

Yes, Jolie thought, but she was smart enough not to say it. "I don't know. You look familiar too."

Kindra smiled when Jolie shook her hand. Her teeth were as bright as stars.

Kindra passed the interview. The slopes flourished under her care. She became known for making the best ski snow in the state, then the region, then the nation.

The first time she fucked Jolie was in the compressor room, the motors thrumming as the machines churned out endless piles of snow onto the slope above.

"Why do I feel like I've done this with you before?" Kindra said, licking Jolie's arousal from her fingers.

Jolie smirked. "Already tired of me?"

"Not that way. The good way—like I've fucked you in a past lifetime. Like I'll fuck you in the next one. And on again, forever. That's how irresistible you are."

"So you're saying we're going to live happily ever after?"

Kindra kissed Jolie, hummed into her mouth. "I believe so."

Dance for Me

"AGAIN!" SHE BARKED, HITTING the tip of her cane against the wooden floor. Its *thunk* reverberated through the boards and made the soles of my feet tingle.

I was exhausted. The muscles in my legs and arms quivered like piano strings. But if she wanted me to do it again, so be it. I would give anything to please her.

The accompanist started playing. Professor Lacey thumped her cane faster, goading him up-tempo until his hands flew across the keys at breakneck speed. I felt momentarily sorry for him, until it hit my consciousness that I would have to keep that pace with my entire body, not just my hands. I returned to my starting position at the center of the room.

I'd been dancing for three hours straight—through the ninety-minute group class and now through my weekly private session. Even after seven semesters at a performing arts school, that much dancing was exhausting.

"Your landings are still too heavy, Miranda. If you get it right this time, we're done for the day."

I sucked in my bottom lip, doubting the laws of physics would allow improvement on this front.

Professor Lacey was fluent in body language, and responded as decisively as if I'd spoken my doubts. "I know you don't think you can do it, but *I* know you can. And you will." It was an order as much as a statement of faith. Her eyes were sharp, focused, alive. I felt my strength returning. My muscles were embers being stoked back into flame.

She tapped the cane against the floor. The movement made her black curls bounce. "On 'four'! One, two, three-and—"

I leapt in the air, then landed as soft as snow. Whether it was the practice or my inability to disobey Professor Lacey's wishes, I couldn't say. I tried not to think about it. Overanalyzing things in the midst of a dance is a sure way to screw up. I surrendered to my body's intelligence and to my teacher: her tapping cane, her commanding voice, the passion she brought to each lesson.

Desire bloomed in my loins. I was flying. I was free.

The dance came to an end. I was on the floor, bent on one knee, my torso pressed against my thigh, my head tucked. I was folded in on myself like a sleeping dove, but my body was supremely awake. I breathed heavily. Blood thrummed through my veins, pounding in my ears. Otherwise, the room was silent.

Clap. Clap. Clap.

I looked up. Professor Lacey had her cane tucked under her elbow so she could slap her palms together.

My mind flashed back to the only other time she'd ever clapped for me. It had been early on in the year, when I'd fought her tooth and nail on everything. She'd wanted me to kick higher. I'd given her a long-winded speech about anatomy and the limitations of my own body. When I'd paused long enough to catch my breath, she'd clapped and said with a sneer, "Brava, Myra. Put that much passion in your acting and maybe someday you'll win a Tony."

Was she mocking me now?

But then I saw her eyes. For the first time since I'd begun working with her, they were alight with unabashed approval. She was smiling so hard it pinched the skin around them into crow's feet. "That was beautiful, Myra. I knew you could do it. We're done for today."

Exhaustion overtook me again, as well as an unfamiliar emotion—relief. I wanted to crawl the distance between us and kiss her feet. Instead, I stood and gave a curtsy.

She walked toward me. Like the piano earlier, my heartbeat went up-tempo. She rested her hand between my sweat-drenched shoulder blades. "Go to bed early tonight. Your body needs to recover."

Dancing was not my forte. I'd been a singer first, and then had discovered musical theater. Acting had come easily to me. Dancing? Not so much. I wasn't terrible at it—as a musician, I had no problem moving in time with a beat. But I danced with proficiency, not artistry. My body was tense and inflexible. High kicks and splits were the bane of my existence. I hated being bandied about in some leading man's arms.

I was now at a school for the performing arts in Manhattan, majoring in musical theater. My first three years hadn't been so tough, since my previous dance professors had let me treat the subject as secondary—an accessory to the things I truly cared about. Professor Lacey wouldn't put up with that attitude. She expected me to dance like it was an end in itself. She wanted me to say as much with my body as I could with my voice.

At first, I'd hated her for it. Didn't she understand there were things I simply couldn't do? Besides, I was destined to be a leading lady, and directors and choreographers constantly make adjustments for their leads' inferior dancing skills. Ethel Merman wasn't expected to be Ginger Rogers. Kristin Chenoweth wasn't Beyoncé.

I'd barged into her office with this argument during the third week of class. I'd just received an email with the grade from my first performance exam with her: D-minus. "This is unacceptable! You're judging me on criteria you'd use for an *actual* dancer. But I'm good enough for musical theater. I know I am!"

My arguments hadn't flown with her. "You don't break into a cut-throat business by being 'good enough.' You do it by blowing people's minds. And that's what I'm going to teach you to do. If you don't want what I'm offering, if it's just too hard for you, talk to your dean. I'm sure she can find some useless filler class to round out your major. You'll have a nice-looking degree to stare at while you wait for calls from your agent that never come."

She'd found my fatal weakness and employed it against me: pride. I was willing to swear eighteen ways to Tuesday that Professor Lacey was unfair in her grading, but no way was I going to admit her class was too hard for me.

So I stuck with it, through all the pain and sweat. I let her break me down, unteaching me the bad habits I'd accumulated through the years. It was the most difficult work of my entire undergraduate career. I learned my body could do things I had never expected. Hannah Lacey pushed me beyond what I thought I was capable of. And I loved her for it.

I developed the habit of doing everything Professor Lacey told me to, and learned that taking her advice was always to my benefit.

So on the nights she told me to go to bed early, I would—though I didn't always fall asleep right away. I was distracted by images from her studio. Her curly black hair framing her brown face. Her whiskey-colored eyes. Her small breasts, snug in her leotard. Her small hands resting on the large brass knob that topped her dancing cane.

She often wore scarves around her neck. I imagined her unwinding one, holding it out to me like an offering. *Come here, Myra,* she'd say. I'd walk over to the grand piano, and she'd have me lie on it, my calves dangling over the back leg. She'd tie the scarf around my ankles, binding me to the piano, and then another scarf would appear in her hands, and she would use that to bind my wrists over my head. Then she'd shove off her wrap skirt and pull the crotch of her leotard aside, sinking onto my face, her hot, wet labia pressed against my lips. *Eat,* she'd say, and of course I would, feasting on her dripping pussy as she moaned and writhed. *Good job, Myra,* she'd moan. *I knew you could do this.* She'd thrust her cunt onto my tongue, her clit against my nose, and as she neared climax she'd reach behind her—a dancer is nothing if not flexible—and slip her fingers into my wetness. She'd come with my name on her lips.

I had some of the best orgasms of my life during these masturbatory sessions, two fingers working furiously over my clit while those of the other hand squeezed at my breasts. They were fierce and overwhelming and, frankly, much more delightful than what Jane, my girlfriend at the time, was giving me. My real sex life was as vanilla as they get. I'd never recognized my own submissive nature until Professor Lacey awoke it. But it didn't occur to me to pursue her. She seemed far off, unreachable. Besides, I was pretty sure it was against the rules.

"Tie me up," I said one evening to Jane. We were in her bed, our clothes halfway off.

She looked at me like I'd gone crazy. "Why would I do that?"

"I just—I thought it would be fun to try. That's all."

To Jane's credit, she tried. But the energy was all wrong. "It feels weird when you can't touch me back," she said. "And how am I supposed to get off?"

"You could sit on my face."

She squinched her nose. "But that's so demeaning."

That's the idea, I wanted to say, but didn't. It wasn't Jane I wanted demeaning me, anyway. It was Professor Lacey. I wanted to give myself over to her completely—not just my dancing, but all of me. I wanted her to take me apart and build me back up again, make me more whole than I was before.

A week before graduation, I went out with a group of friends to celebrate the completion of exams. Jane and I had broken up by then—the vanilla sex had become unbearable to me, and my demands for kink had become unbearable to her— and I was hoping the night would end with me getting laid by a powerful stranger.

I hadn't gotten all my grades back yet, but I knew I'd done well enough that my degree was in no danger. Professor Lacey's class was the most challenging, and even she had given me an approving smile when I finished my routine for her, though this time she had not clapped. "You've grown so much this year," she'd said at the conclusion of my dance. "It's been an honor to watch you bloom."

She was, of course, the reason for my blossoming. She was the sun and rain. Without her, I couldn't have grown.

My desire to find a fuckable stranger flew out the window as soon as my group walked into the bar and I spotted Professor Lacey in the corner, sharing drinks with another woman around her age. Professor Lacey's companion looked like she might be a dancer too, with a wiry body and long blonde hair cascading down her back. The blonde batted her eyes and laughed enthusiastically whenever my professor spoke, but Professor Lacey didn't return the enthusiasm. She seemed distracted. She fiddled with the ends of her own silk scarf, her eyes flitting around the room until, at last, they landed on me.

Her mouth spread into a smile. I waved. She winked at me. My stomach flipped.

She turned back to her companion, and the moment was suddenly gone. I wondered if it had occurred at all. Perhaps it had been a product of my horny imagination.

My friends and I found a table. I had one margarita and then another. My eyes scanned the bar as restlessly as Professor Lacey's had done when I'd first entered. They often wandered to her, and to the blonde, who was ramping up her flirtations. Every few minutes, she reached across the table to readjust Professor Lacey's purple scarf or touch her hand. Jealousy burned my throat.

As I finished my third margarita, Professor Lacey walked over to the bar. The blonde checked her phone, then rifled through a purse for a small mirror, which she peered at in the dim light to apply lipstick.

I slammed my glass down on the table, excused myself to my friends, and made a beeline to the bar.

"Professor Lacey! What a surprise to see you here!" My head felt woozy and my chest warm. These sensations only increased when Professor Lacey turned away from the bartender to face me head on. Her lips curled as if she were trying to stifle a laugh. I didn't know how I felt about that. I liked to see her happy, but I didn't want her laughing at my expense.

"I'm not drunk, if that's what you're thinking. I'm just happy to see you."

Professor Lacey's smile grew. "I'm happy to see you, too. Though usually when people start off a conversation with, 'I'm not drunk,' it means they are."

I was too thrilled by her first statement to be offended by her second. Professor Lacey was happy to see *me*. Perhaps it was the first glimpse of happiness she'd had all night. Perhaps she would take me home with her, and I could give her even more.

The bartender set a drink in front of Professor Lacey. I pulled out my wallet. "Let me buy your drink, professor."

She put a hand on my wrist to stop me from opening the wallet. It was a light touch, but commanding. "No, thank you, Myra. That wouldn't be appropriate. I haven't turned in all your grades yet."

I glanced back at her table as she gave the bartender a ten. The blonde was watching us. I waved, as if to assure her I was no threat, though I hoped I was. An idea popped in my head—one that would satisfy my curiosity about the blonde woman's status, and that might also convince Professor Lacey to accept some sort of gift from me. "Is that your date? I can buy her a drink, instead of you. *She's* not grading me."

"She's not my date. And don't fool yourself into thinking I can't see right through why you asked me that." Her smile disappeared. It turned grim, disciplinary—the way it had always turned when I wasn't performing up to her standards. "I don't fuck my students, Myra."

If she'd slapped me across the face, it would have stung less. But I wasn't going to give up so easily. I reached out and curled my fingers around the end of her scarf. It was one I'd seen many times. Batiked deep purple, it seemed almost as much a part of her body as her brown skin. "I've always thought this scarf would look so pretty tied around my wrists."

I didn't look away from her eyes. There seemed to be a struggle going on behind them, but the rest of her face remained impassive. "Be that as it may, you are still my student and you've had too much to drink."

"I'm not too drunk to know what I want."

"By any legal definition, I'm afraid you are, darling." She took her drink and held it up as if in a toast. "Congratulations on your impending graduation, Myra. I look forward to seeing you on Broadway." She turned and walked back to the blonde.

I collapsed onto a bar stool, my eyes not moving from her though she refused to look my way again. She had called me *darling*. She'd implicitly agreed her scarf would look lovely on my wrists. She thought I was headed for Broadway.

It was the best rejection I'd ever received. I went back to my friends, had a few more drinks, and looked forward to masturbating myself to sleep when I got home. After graduation, I'd make another move on Professor Lacey, and she would say yes.

But when I woke up the next morning with a headache like an axe to the skull, the conversation's meaning seemed altogether different. She hadn't agreed I'd look nice tied up in her scarf; she'd simply avoided disagreeing. Her *darling* had been a dismissal, not an endearment. *I look forward to seeing you on Broadway* wasn't exactly an invitation to keep in close touch. She'd barely held back a sneer.

I'd bought a card to send to her at graduation, to thank her for the ways in which she'd changed my perceptions of my own abilities, for driving me to do better than I'd thought possible.

But what I'd really wanted to say was *I love you and don't want to live without you.*

She could clearly live without me. I threw the card away.

I did my best to forget about her, though it was impossible to let go of her completely. She'd become part of my muscle memory, of the way I moved whenever I danced.

I met women who were willing to tie me up, spank me, flog me, gag me—to push me past the boundaries that had held me in before. I fell in love with none of them, and none of them fell in love with me. When they disciplined me, I often imagined Professor Lacey's voice in place of theirs, her wooden dance cane in place of their whips and riding crops. My body and heart thrived on the attention all the same.

I made it into a Broadway chorus line, then as an understudy for one of the show's supporting cast members. A few months later, I got the call from my agent that would change my life in more ways than one: I'd gotten the lead in an off-off-Broadway musical that was moving to off-Broadway. My agent told me my dancing was what had made me stand out in callbacks.

I was on the bus, squeezed between an old lady with a collapsible grocery cart and a skinny kid who smelled like patchouli. My heart thudded in my chest. Throughout callbacks, I'd pretended I was dancing for Professor Lacey. It was a trick I used frequently in auditions. Picturing her eyes on me, hearing her thumping cane with each beat—they both soothed my nerves and made me perform better than I thought possible.

I had to tell her. I had to thank her. Even if I wasn't a necessary fixture in her life, she had changed mine for the better. Thirty seconds later I was outside, running to the subway, zipping toward Manhattan and my alma mater.

Running back to her.

The building was open when I got there, students milling in the halls. But the studio was empty, and her office door closed.

I knocked.

"Who is it?" It was her voice, clear and self-possessed as always.

"Myra Jamison."

A chair screeched against the wooden floor. A lock tumbled. The door opened.

Professor Lacey looked exactly as I remembered her—leotard snug to her subtle curves, the purple silk scarf from that night at the bar, a skirt wrapped around her boyish hips.

She also looked nothing like I remembered. The expression on her face was one I had never seen before—pained and straining, like she was fighting back hope. She held herself rigidly, inflexible as the dance cane that leaned against the wall, its spherical brass handle glinting in the window's light. "Myra, come in." Her breath was fast, shallow. She gestured for me to sit on the couch and locked the door behind me. "It's good to see you. Surprising, but good."

I didn't sit. I couldn't. Adrenaline pounded in my veins. "Professor Lacey—"

"Call me Hannah. You're not a student anymore." That kind of invitation ought to be filled with warmth, but her voice and eyes were cold.

"Hannah. I got a musical lead. Off-Broadway. And I wanted to thank you, because I never did—"

Her cold demeanor evaporated. She threw her arms around me—the first time she'd ever done so—and pulled me close. I felt her breasts against mine, her heart beating against my ribcage. She kissed my cheek. "There's nothing to thank me for. You did all the work."

"I only did the work because you dared me to." I tried to shrug the kiss off as a meaningless gesture, but my body didn't get the memo. It thrummed with electricity and desire. I turned my face instinctively, pressing my lips against hers.

She responded immediately, opening her mouth, sucking hard on my bottom lip, then tugging it between her teeth. I moaned, clutching my hands around her shoulders like she was a life preserver. Soon she had me pressed against the desk, her hands curling into my ass. My hips stuttered. Something fell clattering to the floor.

Hannah startled back. "Myra—" She was breathless.

"Don't stop kissing me." I tugged at the ends of her scarf. She stepped toward me—not unwillingly, but not eagerly, either. Her face was a question mark. "Please, Professor…Hannah. I've wanted you ever since I stopped hating you."

Her mouth quirked into a smile. "You really did hate me for a while, didn't you?"

I nodded. "Until I realized I needed the guidance of someone who was willing to break me." I looked into her dark, unblinking eyes. "I still do. Do you want to do that for me, Hannah? May I submit myself to you?"

"Oh, god, yes." She surged toward me, closing the last inches between us, her delicate dancer's fingers on my jaw and neck. "I've wanted that with you since *before* you stopped hating me."

I would have laughed, but her lips were against

mine, almost violent in their need. She pried my teeth open with her tongue, pushed herself into my mouth—took me, possessed me. Her hands were everywhere: my face and neck, my hair, my breasts, my ass. She tugged at the hem of my sweater and pulled it up, revealing the utilitarian beige bra beneath. I cursed myself for not planning ahead, but my shame didn't last long. She tugged it off along with the shirt and threw them both to the floor, taking one breast in her hand and pulling my nipple into her mouth with a hard suck.

Pleasure shot to my toes. I yelped my approval.

"There are people in the hallway, Myra. Am I going to have to gag you?"

"Yes, do, please," I whispered breathlessly, my arousal ratcheting up past its earlier limits.

Hannah smirked and stepped back. "Fine, then. But I don't have any gags at the ready here. We'll have to improvise." With that, she hauled me onto the desk, pulling down my jeans and panties so that I was stripped bare, my back and ass against the cool wood, the rest of me exposed to the air. Goosebumps prickled on my skin.

"Before I gag you—" She leaned over me, kissing me fiercely as I wrapped my bare legs around her waist, pressing my clit against her pubic bone. Through the fabric of her leotard, I felt her nipples growing hard and pebbled against my own breasts.

I tugged again at her scarf. "Please, professor. Don't you think this scarf would look better tied around my wrists?"

"You vixen," she muttered into my neck. "Do you know how hard it was not to take you that night at the bar? The way you looked at me—you were practically begging for it."

"Not *practically*. I *was* begging for it. I wanted you to fuck me, professor. I wanted you to own me."

"And don't think I don't notice you 'professor'-ing me. I know what you're up to."

"What am I up to?" I thrust my clit against her pubic bone again, seeking more friction.

"You're playing the pervy little schoolgirl, Myra. Are you looking for a spanking?"

"I can't say I'd mind one."

She slid down and walked around the desk, slipping off her scarf. "Wrists above your head, my darling." Wetness gushed from my cunt at the endearment, and again at the feeling of her silk scarf pressing against my wrists. She made the binding snug but not overly tight—she was clearly experienced at this—then pressed something cold and metallic into one of my palms. "Keys," she said in response to my questioning look. "Drop them if you need to stop. Because you won't be able to say 'red' around these." She lifted my panties to my face. They smelled strongly of my arousal. "This is your gag, my darling Myra. Now open your mouth and bite down." I did. The silken fabric was wet and slick. I wished it was her I tasted, and not me. Perhaps she would give me that gift later, if I was good for her.

"Now spread your legs. I want to get a good view of your beautiful cunt. I've wanted to taste it since you first back-talked me."

I planted my feet wide on the desk, my knees in the air. I felt deliciously exposed as she traced the tips of her fingers over my labia. I bit into my panties to keep from grunting out my pleasure. "What a juicy pink pussy, Myra. So wet for me. Did you always get this wet when you performed for me?" She slid two fingers into my desperate cunt. "Watching you dance always got me wet, darling— seeing you work so hard for my approval. Sometimes I'd have to come here into my office and fuck myself afterward just to get on with the day."

I churned my hips, seeking friction against my G-spot.

"Not yet, darling. I need to tell you something else. You know my dancing cane?"

I nodded against the desk.

"Can you guess how many times I've gotten off to the thought of fucking you with the brass handle? Would you like that, darling? Would you like to polish it with your cunt?"

I moaned around my wadded panties. That cane was as much a part of her as her hand or tongue. To have it inside my body, filling and stretching me, would be a dream come true. I spread my legs a little more, and she worked three fingers in.

"I bet you've dreamed about me disciplining you with it, too, haven't you? I saw the way you used to look at it, darling, like you were afraid of it and wanted it at the same time. Was I reading you right, sweet Myra?"

I nodded again, groaning around the gag. I lifted my ass off the table, ready to expose myself to her beatings.

She merely gave it a light slap—a promise of pain rather than the thing itself. "Not today. Right now, I want to make love to you. Will you let me do that?"

I answered by fucking myself onto her fingers. She curled the pads against my G-spot, rubbing it in smooth, irresistible circles. My cunt spasmed; my eyes rolled back in my head. I was right on the edge of coming, if only she would press her thumb to my clit or pinch my nipple with her free hand.

Instead, she slipped her fingers out. "I'm not letting you come yet, darling. I haven't waited this long to fuck you for it to be all over."

She stepped back. I craned my neck to watch her. She unwrapped the skirt from her waist and dropped it to the floor, then unpeeled her leotard and tights from her skin. Beneath them was a black cotton bra and panties, which she left on as she grabbed the cane from its resting place by the wall. She smoothed her hands over the brass globe at the top before stretching it out to me, rolling it over my nipples and belly, my ass and thighs, my neck and arms. The metal was cold at first, but grew less so as she soothed it over my skin. I closed my eyes and luxuriated in the sensation. It was as sensual as kisses, as erotic as a lover's tongue exploring the crevices of my body. Each touch made me shiver with longing, made my cunt grow hungrier with desire.

"Take me", I tried to beg around the panties in my mouth, but the words came out as a garbled moan.

"You'd like me to fuck you, wouldn't you, Myra? You feel like you can't possibly stand another minute without something in your cunt."

I nodded desperately, close to tears.

She rolled the handle over my gaping pussy lips—a tease more than a relief. "I think you can stand it, Myra. If I ask you to stand it, you'll rise to the occasion, won't you?"

I took a deep breath, let her will become my own. I kept my hips still as she continued to roll the knob over my labia, coating it in my juices. I willed my cunt not to quiver, not even when she added to the torture by dipping her head down and sucking my hard nipple into an even harder peak. "Oh, Myra," she moaned, "your tits are to die for."

The compliment made me flush and forget my own desire. So when the brass sphere pushed suddenly into my pussy, it was a shock bordering on revelation. I spasmed hungrily around it, pulling it in until the cool brass nuzzled my G-spot. Tears of ecstasy streamed down my face. I grasped the keys so tightly the teeth cut into my skin—but better that than dropping them to the floor. There was no way I was going to let that happen now, not when Hannah had me right where she wanted me.

She wiped the tears from my cheeks. "You're doing so well, sweetheart. I'll let you come soon. But first, I want to take this gag out of your mouth and replace it with my cunt. Would you like that?"

I nodded eagerly, holding back my whimper as she pulled the cane's brass knob from my cunt and licked it like a lollipop. "You taste like honey, Myra. Do you want to know what I taste like?" She removed the gag.

"Yes, professor. Please. Please let me taste your cunt." She stood up to remove her panties and bra. Her nipples were as dark as her eyes and bigger than silver dollars. My mouth watered at the sight, but I was soon distracted by something even more tempting as she climbed onto the desk, her knees on either side of my shoulders and her face resting against my raised knee. Her cunt hovered about a foot above my face, its lips engorged and glistening with arousal. I struggled to lift my head so I could taste it, but with my wrists tied above me, it was impossible to get enough purchase.

"Patience," Hannah chided as she inserted the brass globe back into my cunt.

"Oh god!"

"Shhhh."

"I'd be quieter if you sat on my face," I muttered.

"You do have a point." She sank down, aligning her cunt over my outstretched tongue, grinding her clit against my chin. She smelled of sweat and tasted like sugar and butter, melting just as easily on my probing tongue. "Yes, Myra, eat me just like that." She bit my knee with a stifled cry.

Her clit swelled against my chin. I pulled my tongue from her cunt and lapped it down over her hard nub, sweeping back and forth between the two, aided by her vigorous rocking. Inside my own cunt, the brass sphere seemed to be spinning against my G-spot. I quivered around it, ready to melt.

"Myra," she muttered, "I'm so close. Do you want to come with me?"

I couldn't answer except by fucking her more vigorously with my tongue and working myself over the brass sphere.

Suddenly her tongue was on my clit, lapping eagerly as she continued to press her cunt into my face. Her labia fluttered, and then her whole body. She moaned, sending sparks up my spine. I cried into her cunt, coming with my whole body as she gushed creamy wetness into my mouth and over my chin.

I came for what seemed like ages, my body refusing to stop even as she pulled the brass handle from inside me and dropped it to the floor. "Not bad for our first time together," she said as she rolled off and rearranged herself so she was lying next to me on the wide desk, her head pressed against my shoulder. "I can't wait to see what our second time is like. And the times after that."

I kissed her. Our juices mingled on our tongues.

"I probably have a hundred fantasies I'd like to try out with you, if it wouldn't be a bother."

She smiled. "Do any of them involve me fucking you in the dance studio? Because I have one about tying you to the baby grand that I'd love to try sometime, now that you're no longer my student."

I smiled. "Great minds think alike."

In a Pinch

THEIR APARTMENT IS A SHOEBOX, but it's what they can afford on their grad school stipends, so Nicole is mostly happy with it even if it means they can't fit a full couch in the living-slash-dining room that also serves as an office. Nicole half sits, half lies on the loveseat with a big, floppy pillow under her back and her legs bent into upside-down Vs. Her socked feet are planted firmly on the loveseat cushion, but as she turns the next page in Katherine Mansfield's *Collected Stories*, she stretches one leg out, propping her calf against the armrest and letting her foot dangle freely in the air.

She enjoys the feeling of being at her full length, even though she also knows the pressure of the armrest will eventually cut off her circulation and her ankle and foot will go pins-and-needles numb. She hates that sensation.

She keeps her leg outstretched anyway and keeps

reading. The shower running in the bathroom a few feet away serves as the perfect, rainy backdrop for the story in which she's immersed.

Nicole doesn't notice when the shower shuts off. The sound of Jess moving around in the bathroom—humming to herself, opening and shutting drawers, picking up and setting down lotion bottles, snapping the towel in the air before hanging it to dry—is just as familiar and soothing.

That is, until Jess's voice snaps as sharply as the towel. "Fuck!"

Nicole jolts up straight. Jess doesn't swear often outside the bedroom.

"You okay, Jess?"

There's a slight delay before Jess answers. "Um, yeah." Something metal clinks against the tile counter. Nail clippers? A barrette? "Just ... grooming. I'm fine."

"Okay." Nicole turns back to her reading, but only gets two sentences further before a stifled hiss seeps through the bathroom door. It's similar to the sound Jess makes when she waxes her legs, but that can't be what's going on in there. Nicole hasn't heard the distinctive *rrrriiip* that the wax-soaked cotton strips always make as Jess pulls them from her skin, like one piece of Velcro pulling away from another.

The medicine cabinet opens and closes again, followed by a silent pause and another hiss.

"Jess? Do you need help in there?"

"I don't ... think so. No. No. I'm fine."

Nicole tries to accept the answer. Her natural tendency is to run and rescue anyone at the earliest sign of distress, but she's learned the hard way that's not always what people want or need. With Jess especially. Jess is an introvert and staunchly independent. Sharing a tiny apartment has forced them to learn how to give each other space when they need it. Jess's showering ritual is her solitary time.

Besides, Nicole got most of her caretaking urges out earlier today during her twice-weekly shift at the animal shelter. She buries her nose back in her book.

A sudden pig-squeal noise makes the hairs in Nicole's ears stand on end.

"Okay, I know it's none of my business, but what are you trying to do in there? Give yourself a tattoo?" It's a ridiculous question. Jess is one of the most vanilla people Nicole knows when it comes to…everything—sex, clothes, body modification. They've never gotten any kinkier than using a strap-on. Most of Jess's clothes are beige or cream. She wouldn't be caught dead in stilettos, and she doesn't even have pierced ears. She told Nicole once that she'd thought about getting them when she was twelve, but wimped out. She couldn't stop worrying about them getting caught on something and ripping her earlobes in half.

Jess chortles. "No. Definitely not a tattoo."

"Well, whatever it is doesn't sound pleasant."

"It's not, exactly. I wouldn't call it unpleasant,

though." Jess's voice starts as singsong, but ends on a low note that she usually reserves for when she's seducing Nicole.

"What's that supposed to mean?"

Jess opens the bathroom door a crack—just enough to let a little of the soap-and-shampoo scent leak into the living room, but not enough that Nicole can actually see inside. "You can come in and watch if you're that curious."

Well. Nicole's not going to turn down a direct invitation. She sets the book on the loveseat and walks the three steps to the bathroom. She pushes the door open.

Jess is standing naked in front of the mirror, her wide hips and pendulous breasts on lavish display. Nicole forgets why she's there. Her eyes flit back and forth between Jess and her reflection; they're both so sexy.

It's muggy like a rainforest in here, though the mirror is no longer fogged. Nicole pushes her sleeves up past her elbows, feels sweat bloom under her arms and in the crotch of her jeans. The wetness makes her think of other kinds of wetness, and soon she's sidling up behind Jess, her hands around Jess's hips, admiring the way they look together in the mirror.

Nicole notices the pair of tweezers in Jess's hand.

"You're plucking? But your eyebrows are perfect already," Nicole says.

Jess doesn't say anything, just smiles knowingly,

like she's privy to some secret.

"What?"

Jess's smile grows wider. Her cheeks flush. "It wasn't my eyebrows." She pulls her plump lower lip into her mouth, her top teeth blanching her pink skin. "It was my nipples."

Nicole involuntarily curls her fingers into her palms so hard that she can feel her nails etching half-moons into her skin. She's plucked the hairs around her areolas before and it stings like a bitch—and hers are fine and feathery, not the thick, wiry threads that sprout from Nicole's skin. "That hurts just to think about," Nicole says. "You know I like your body just as it is, right?"

"Yeah. But I'm not doing it for you. I'm doing it because it's … interesting."

"What do you mean, interesting?"

Jess half-shrugs and turns toward the mirror. She lifts the tweezers to her breast, clasping a thick black hair between its prong tips. She holds the skin taut with her other hand as she tugs, her breath still, her cheeks growing pinker as the hair eases out of her body. She winces as it pulls free, and then gasps. It's a high, wispy noise, not unlike the ones she makes when Nicole makes that first, gentle lick across Jess's clitoris when she eats her out.

The root is white and at least twice as thick as the hair itself. "Damn," says Nicole. "That must be excruciating."

"It is. But it's also … intoxicating. Here, you try it." Jess holds the tweezers out for Nicole to take.

"I'd rather not."

"Not on you, silly. On me. Pull one out. I want to know what it feels like when I'm not in control."

Nicole scrunches her nose, but she doesn't see any reason not to comply with the request, even if it's against her instincts to intentionally cause Jess pain. It's not like Jess is asking to be injured or maimed.

Nicole accepts the tweezers.

Jess closes her eyes as Nicole presses the thumb and forefinger of her left hand to Jess's breast and uses them to stretch the skin tight. With the tweezers in her right hand, she carefully grips the base of a dark, curly hair on the north pole of Jess's areola. Nicole draws it out slowly but steadily, feeling the resistance, watching the skin peak like a small hill around the hair's base until Jess lets out a low hiss and the hair comes free.

"Again," Jess whispers.

Nicole moves on to the next hair, and then the next. Jess's blush creeps down her throat and across her collarbones. Her nipples grow hard and round as cherry pits. "Another one," she pleads when Nicole's reduced the dozen or so hairs around Jess's right nipple to a handful.

Nicole goes until the skin there is bare, then moves to Jess's left breast. Jess shifts her legs and the scent of her arousal wafts up into the air. She must be very wet for Nicole to be able to smell her so soon after a shower.

Nicole feels her own arousal grow. It starts in

her clit, as solid and dense as a seed, then unfurls in warm tendrils down her mons and up into her cunt until even her cervix feels flushed and needy. She needs Jess between her legs and inside her, and needs to be inside Jess just as much. She longs to slip a finger into Jess's folds, to bury herself in Jess's slick heat.

But she has a job to finish.

Nicole grasps two neighboring hairs and pulls both at once.

"Oh fuck!" Jess gasps. Her eyes open. Her pupils are dark and wide. She grabs Nicole and kisses her hard, her teeth sharp against Nicole's lips, her tongue a force to be reckoned with.

Nicole pulls back, a smirk forming on her lips. "Does that mean you liked it?"

"It hurt so fucking much," Jess pants. "I loved it."

"Then let me try again." Nicole grasps two more hairs and pulls them out simultaneously. The rest of the hairs are spaced too far apart to repeat the trick, but Nicole has an idea—something she's never tried before with anyone, though she's read enough erotic romance to know some people are into this. Given Jess's response to pain so far, it's worth a try.

Nicole continues to hold the skin of Jess's breast taut between her thumb and forefinger, but now curls her other three fingers under so Jess's nipple is caught between the back of Nicole's middle and ring fingers. As Nicole yanks out the next hair, she squeezes the curled fingers together to give Jess's nipple a sharp tweak.

Jess's groan rumbles straight into Nicole's belly. "Good?" Nicole says, although she knows the answer already.

"So good. I had no idea—" Whatever Jess was about to say gets broken off by another moan. Jess crosses her legs, the muscles in her thighs going tense as Nicole moves on to the last hair. "I'm so turned on right now."

"You want me to fuck you when we're done?"

"Yes. I also want this to never be done."

Nicole pulls out the final hair, then pinches both of Jess's nipples hard. "It doesn't have to be." She guides Jess so that her ass is flush with the bathroom counter. Jess gets the hint. She lifts herself onto the tiles, letting her legs fall open while Nicole drops knees-first to the floor.

"Take off your shirt so I can feel you," Jess says.

Nicole licks a stripe up the center of Jess's spread labia. "That's not feeling enough?" she teases.

"Never."

Nicole pulls her shirt off over her head and tosses it to the floor, but she's too eager to eat Jess to bother with her jeans. Those stay on, the center seam applying a pleasant pressure on Nicole's cunt as she sinks her mouth back into Jess's folds.

Nicole's hand crawls up to pinch Jess's nipple.

"Oh god!" Jess's cry ricochets against the bathroom walls, urging Nicole on. Nicole licks deeper into Jess, her chin already drenched in juice, her nostrils filled with Jess's scent. She probes her tongue into Jess's hungry cunt and gives another hard squeeze.

"Fuck!" Jess's thighs quiver, her calves swinging back and forth like windshield wipers over Nicole's back as her excitement mounts. She seems just a hair's breadth away from orgasm.

Nicole draws her tongue to Jess's clit, licking tight circles around it as she works two fingers into Jess's wet cunt and then curls the fingertips against the spot that always makes Jess fall apart.

With the other hand, she twists Jess's nipple halfway around until left is right and top is bottom.

Jess doesn't cry out. She stops making any sound at all. She holds her breath as her back arches violently and her thighs shake, then suddenly go rigid. Her cunt pulses around Nicole's fingers, pushing juice out onto her waiting tongue. It always tastes slightly different when Jess is coming—more watery but also somehow headier.

Jess gasps, her spine collapsing toward the counter. She pulls Nicole up from between her thighs. "Now take off your jeans, baby. I'm not done with you yet."

They move to the bedroom. Nicole's clothes come off and Jess works one end of their double dildo into Nicole's waiting cunt.

"Can I try something?" Nicole is overcome by a

sudden urge to test the extent of Jess's desire for pain.

Jess hovers over her, her hair falling around Nicole's face, shutting out the world around them. "Surprise me."

Nicole pulls Jess closer. Jess is ticklish right beneath her earlobe, and Nicole wonders—

She bites down on the skin.

"Oh!" Jess twists the dildo inside Nicole's body.

"Is that a 'do that again,' or 'never do that again'?"

"Definitely 'do that again.' But not until I get the harness on you. I need you to fuck me, babe."

Nicole chuckles. "You're insatiable."

"That's why you love me."

"Harder, harder, please, harder." Jess is on her knees, her back against Nicole's chest, her hands white-knuckling the headboard, and she's begging in the way that Nicole loves, even if Nicole's not sure what needs to be harder: the fucking, or the squeeze around Jess's nipples, or the bite of Nicole's teeth into her skin.

So Nicole goes for all three. She thrusts her hips hard and fast against Jess's ass, feels the tight pull of Jess's cunt on the dildo; pinches and twists Jess's proud nipples; bites into Jess's shoulders until her teeth leave purple marks in the skin.

"Jesus fuck, I've needed this for so long, Nicole,

wanted—" Her words devolve into a sharp cry.

"For how long?" Nicole says, wrenching Jess's nipples in the other direction. Jess lets out another bark.

"Feels like forever, except I didn't know, like it was in me but I didn't know it's name and—*oh Nicole god yes that*," Jess hisses in response to Nicole's teeth on her earlobe.

Nicole fucks Jess frantically, the inner end of the dildo slams against Nicole's cervix with each thrust. She feels herself turning into jelly, knows she's going to come soon if she doesn't slow down. Jess can come a million times, but Nicole's almost always done after one or two, and she can feel already that the approaching one is going to be a game-ender, hitting her so hard she won't be able to move beyond it to the next crest.

Nicole slips her right hand between the harness and her skin to hold her end of the dildo still while the other end continues to hammer Jess. It's an awkward position, making it impossible to squeeze both of Jess's nipples at once. She almost loses her balance when she tries to put her fingers on Jess's other breast.

"Here, baby, I'll take care of it." Jess plants her head into the pillows to take the weight of her upper body and squeezes her own fingers around her nipples. "Just focus on fucking me."

So Nicole does—at least at first. She pounds the strap-on into Jess, thrusting her deeper into the pillows. She makes up for her inability to twist

Jess's nipples by biting hard at the base of Jess's neck like a cat in heat.

But even with holding the strap-on, she's too close to coming. Impulsively, she does the only thing she can think of to stop the wave of pleasure from cresting: she uses her free hand to grapple at her own tit, twisting its tip suddenly, mercilessly, until the pain is so intense she can barely feel anything else.

"Oh, fuck, baby," Jess cries, her hips swaying over the silicone dick, making it twist inside Nicole despite her best efforts. And suddenly the pain pounding through Nicole's breast becomes hot and exhilarating. It sears Nicole to her core.

Nicole lets go of the dildo and she thrusts forward, letting it rebound inside her as she plunges into Jess. She squeezes and twists both of her own areolas as the toy slams against her cervix.

Jess mutters a string of curses and encouragements.

"You ready to come again, Jess?" Nicole pants.

"Yes, baby. Make me come."

Blood rushes back painfully into Nicole's nipples when she lets go. It's just enough discomfort to keep her aware of her surroundings and focused on Jess's rising orgasm instead of her own. She skates her hands around Jess's torso, sliding them under Jess's hands to cup her breasts and clamp down on the swollen areolas.

"Come for me," Nicole growls, nipping at Jess's ear. "Now."

Jess cries out and fucks herself on the toy with relentless force. Her earlier orgasm was quiet and still. This one is ear shattering. Jess's shout rips through the air and makes the glass in the ceiling lamp ring. Nicole's isn't much quieter. Pleasure radiates out from her cervix in steady waves. She can't remember ever coming so hard before.

They're both too sensitive to keep the dildo inside of them when they're done. Jess uses her pelvic muscles to push her end out and helps Nicole undo the harness. They throw the entire contraption on the floor to deal with later, forgetting about it as soon as it's out of sight. Jess pulls Nicole close, their sweaty breasts mashed together. The air is redolent with the smell of sex. Nicole loves it.

"That was a nice new discovery," she says. "How long have you been keeping that secret?"

Jess sighs into Nicole's neck. "Honestly, I didn't realize I was. I mean, I always knew I got an endorphin rush from waxing and tweezing, and sometimes I got a little turned on. But I didn't know if the turn-on was the pain or the smooth skin."

"And now you know?"

Jess nods and the tip of her nose rubs against Nicole's skin. "There's something empowering about feeling pain and knowing that it won't actually hurt you."

"Huh. I hadn't thought of it that way." Nicole looks down at Jess's swollen areola. "Too bad hair only grows so fast. It'll be a while until I can tweeze you again."

"Yes, but...," Jess says, circling the pad of her index finger softly over Nicole's irritated nipple, "we could make room in this month's budget for a pair of nipple clamps."

"Or maybe," Nicole says, wincing at the touch, "we should invest in two."

Alien Vibes

THE SMOOTH, STAINLESS steel wand gleams in the light from our kitchen window. I can't resist the urge to reach out and touch.

"Do you like it?" you ask, eyebrow quirked. You release your grasp on the T-shaped handle so I can feel the wand's full weight in my hand. At just six inches long and less than an inch in diameter, it's surprisingly heavy. It seems almost as dense as the lead musket balls I carry on my belt during steampunk cosplay. I wonder if it's solid steel all the way through, or if it has a denser metal at its core.

"What is it?" I say. Your profession is metal sculpting, but in your free time you're always designing something new—often for cosplay, although sex toys are another of your talents. Is this apparatus for either of those applications, or perhaps both? I certainly wouldn't mind feeling its solid length between my legs.

"If I told you, I'd be taking all the fun out of this game," you say. "I'm more interested in what *you* think it is."

I consider. Its highly polished surface makes me think of medical labs and hospital equipment. Its weight, on the other hand, makes it seem magical and otherworldly. I turn it over to study the handle. It features something that looks like a trigger, plus ergonomic grooves that seem destined for fingers—except they're spaced too far apart to accommodate the average human hand comfortably. Plus, there are five of them, instead of the standard four. So it's not for humans or any of our primate cousins. That leaves one option. "Is it an alien artifact?"

You wink flirtatiously. "You'll need to be more specific to win the prize."

"Is it used for research on humans?" We're both big fans of the Roswell aliens and all their cultural permutations, from *Close Encounters of the Third Kind* to *Communion* to *Alien Autopsy*. I've always loved the *X-Files* episodes where subjects lie immobile on tables as thin, genderless aliens with bulbous heads, hairless gray skin, and huge black eyes experiment on them. The scenarios are designed to frighten, and they do. But they also leave me aroused. Being held to a table with shiny metal cuffs and having my nether regions prodded while a dozen pairs of black, baseball-sized eyes coldly observe the proceeding—that's been my go-to fantasy as long as I can remember.

You touch a finger to the metal wand. "Can you guess what kind of research?"

My thighs quiver. I want the thing inside me. I soothe my palm over its rounded tip. "It makes me think of an anal probe."

You smirk. "You say that with such certainty. Have you been probed before?"

I bite my lip, feigning timidity as I shake my head—a lie if I ever told one. None of my holes are virgin. "All I know is that I've been abducted. But the memories are so hazy. And I don't ... I don't think that thing could fit inside me."

"You'd be surprised at what aliens can accomplish with their technology."

Heat seeps between my legs. My opening is damp and my clit rock-hard. "Well, if the research has to be done ..." I say tentatively, then clear my throat to shift to a more confident tone. I look into your eyes. "I'll make that sacrifice. For humanity."

I rest on the couch while you summon your alien friend. I've undressed and covered myself with a blanket, but though my eyes are closed, I don't fall asleep. The sounds coming from the bedroom are too titillating. I wonder what you're working on first: transforming our nest into the inside of a spaceship, or transforming yourself.

You've had the perfect costume for these occasions ever since our first trip to the Roswell

UFO Festival. It took you two weeks to assemble the head alone, from mold-making to rubber-pouring to painting. A microphone placed on the interior alters the pitch of your voice and adds an eerie, hollow echo.

The body was easier to construct, since Roswells are shaped roughly like humans, with two arms, two legs and a torso in the center. You found the ideal fabric for the skin—supple like suede, but with a surface as smooth and unvaried as latex.

When you entered the convention center, several festival attendees ran in fright. Me? I stayed close to you, barely able to keep my hands off your smooth gray skin or your nailless six-fingered hands. That night when we got back to our hotel room, you fucked me with those long, lithe fingers until I was ready to take the entirety of your alien hand inside my cunt. Your cold, impassive alien gaze filled me with both exhilaration and fear. I came so hard I saw stars.

I like to call you Zeta when you don the costume, after Zeta Reticula, the binary star system where the Roswell grays are said to originate. I call you by this single name, even though I'm not certain you're the same alien each time. Most Roswell grays look identical to the human eye. Perhaps dozens of aliens have ravished me by now; perhaps only one.

You never call me by name. I'm merely a test subject.

Footsteps, so light they're almost silent, approach. A cool hand touches my arm. A strange, otherworldly voice speaks: "Human, come with me."

I open my eyes. Your huge black ones are right in my face. I'm under your thrall, incapable of any movement you haven't commanded. You tie a blindfold around my eyes and spin me around until I'm dizzy, then pull me after you. We've only gone about twenty steps when you lift me onto a cold metal surface, guiding me to lay supine against it. There's a focused light just above my face, so bright I can see it through my blindfold. I feel the cool press of the restraints as you pull them against my forehead and arms, grow more aroused when I hear them click shut. Your five-fingered, one-thumbed hands press tape against my nipples (electrodes, I hope) then lift my legs up and apart. I'm surprised when you rest them on cool metal stirrups somehow suspended above the table—this feature of the table is new. You lock each leg in place with metal cuffs that kiss my ankles. I moan in anticipation, then catch myself. I shift to a whimper of fear.

Spread open and bared, I must be quite a sight to your alien eyes. Are you a different alien than those who have examined me before? Is this your first time seeing my openings on flagrant display?

"What are you going to do to me, Zeta?" I say,

giving a half-hearted struggle against the restraints.

"We always follow protocol," you say cryptically.

When the last cuff is in place, you remove my blindfold. The light a few inches above my face is blinding, at least twice as bright as the halogen lamps at the dentist's office. With my forehead strapped in place, I can't move to avoid it. I can only roll my eyes away and focus on the darkness outside its halo. A black dot hovers in the center of my vision, a temporary imprint left behind by the lamp.

As my eyes adjust, I notice more than one pair of dark eyes looking down on me from around the table. They stare at me, unblinking, their heads bobbing lightly. One, two … I continue the count and forget to keep breathing. There are so many eyes, I'm dizzy with them.

"Oxygen levels low. Primitive respiratory system. Human must inhale." You grab my thigh and give me a shake. My diaphragm lowers instinctively and a gust of air enters my lungs. The dizziness fades.

I start my count again, forcing deep, even breaths as I go. I count six alien faces on my right side, five on my left—though, light-blind and unable to move my head, I can't be sure of the count. Zeta is at the end of the table, peering between my legs.

A pearl of wetness drips from my front opening. "Zeta." My voice is shaking. It's mostly arousal, but a bit of unease, too. This is something new, something I've only fantasized about. "You aren't alone."

"We're never alone," you say. "Our minds are connected."

"But—" I stammer. The heat rises in my chest and pools in my thighs. "Physically, I mean. In past experiments, only one of you has been physically present."

"True. But many of us always watch you, even if through only one pair of eyes. Your physical responses enlighten our race, human."

"Oh?" I take this as a compliment and blush.

"Yes. We must conduct additional experiments to learn more." With no other preamble, you press the tip of the wand against my asshole. It feels much colder than it did earlier in my hands, a fact emphasized by the generous slathering of lube you've given it. It reminds me of the coldness of outer space. My pucker spasms, instinctively resisting the impending intrusion.

You wait. You've studied humans long enough to know what will happen if you do. We're predictable creatures with predictable bodies. So primitive.

Seconds pass, maybe a minute, before the muscles of my back opening give up the fight. The spasming fades into deep relaxation. My ass opens to your probe.

You push. The probe's tip sinks in. My muscles recover and pulse around it—whether to push it out or pull it in, I can't tell. The sensation is both uncomfortable and delicious. My groan is both agony and joy.

You sink the probe further in, past the internal ring of muscle that guards my depths.

"Fuck!" I pant. If I weren't restrained, the shock of the sensation would arch my back. Sharp bursts of pleasure shoot up my spine. All discomfort is gone now. I want the probe in all the way. I struggle against the restraints, trying to pull it in. I need you to fuck me with it. Now.

"Be still, human!" Your tone is scolding, but not angry. I've never seen you, as Zeta, express a stronger emotion than slight displeasure. You are cool, diffident, and hard to provoke. You seem not to care about anything but following procedure. Whether your experiments arouse or terrify me, it's all the same to you.

There's something liberating about that. I'm free of expectations.

The thought sends blood rushing to my groin, and I instinctively struggle again, rolling my hips against the restraints, trying to deepen the probe's reach into my body.

Your voice grows cold. "Disobedience is futile, human. We are the superior race. We are in command. Struggle again, and we may have to switch to another experiment." You pull the probe from my ass—a sudden, swift movement that leaves me feeling hollow. My anus contracts against the emptiness, as if its desire could force you to fill it back up.

Of course it can't. You aren't like a human.

Desire has no effect on you.

You walk around the table, stepping forward between two of the other aliens in my peripheral vision until I can see your expressionless face clearly. You lift something from a tray beside the table and hold it above my face, blocking the worst of the light from the lamp above with your large hand so I can see the instrument clearly. It's shaped like your own alien finger, but instead of being rounded at the tip, it ends in a metallic claw. You lower it to my bicep and trace circles with the claw's dull underside. "Are you ready to obey?"

I shiver. I'm tempted to defy you, to coax you into scratching a smooth, shallow line into my skin as a souvenir of this abduction. But I want the anal probe even more. "Yes," I groan. It takes all my will not to move.

You set the claw instrument aside and move back between my legs, and without preamble thrust the probe in. I cry out in shock. It's somehow just as cold as it was on its first entry, and that makes me desperately hot. Sweat breaks out on my groin and chest as my ass pulses around the intrusion, trying to pull it deeper even though it's smoothly polished surface leaves nothing to grab onto.

"Notice how the human perspires," you say to your colleagues at either side the table.

A rumble of sinister *ah*s and *We see*s fills my head, each with a slightly different tone. My eyes flicker around, trying to focus on any particular face among my alien audience, trying to figure out which ones of them are speaking. They're just far enough out of my main field of vision that they all remain blurry—all except you, who seem to be smiling in satisfaction, even though your small slit of a mouth hasn't moved.

"Let us see if we can make the human perspire more." You slide the probe in deeper, millimeter by slow millimeter. It's like I'm being fucked by a popsicle that refuses to melt, and the unusual weight of the probe becomes more obvious as more of it sinks into my body. I've never had anything this heavy or cold inside me. The unusual feeling sparks an intense desire for more, but you keep your torturously slow pace. "Human, tell us, how do you feel?"

"Strange," I grunt. "Nervous. Awesome."

You hold the probe still. "These are not objective descriptions, human. Please elaborate."

"Um, I'm aroused."

"Yes, we observe this. Nipples erect, blood flow to the surface of the face and chest, erectile tissue plump and stiff—" You nudge my clitoris. "We recognize these as common signs of arousal. But we do not understand what creates this state. Tell us."

"I like being stretched open. I like how cold and heavy it is. I like its friction against my rim."

"Your 'rim'? Do you mean your anal sphincters?"

"Yes, Zeta. But most humans don't consider that phrase to be very romantic."

"Romance?" you say. "I do not understand."

"Never mind."

"Tell us one more thing about these sensations. Then we will recommence." You give the probe a small, teasing twist that makes my whole body shudder.

"I'm sensitive, inside and out. Movement is very arousing."

"Like this?" you say, angling the probe slightly and pulling it slightly out, then sinking it back in.

"Oh, Zeta!" I let out a guttural cry. "Exactly … exactly like that."

The probe seems to warm slightly with each movement, but never enough for me to forget its coolness or alienness. I breathe deep and try not to struggle, though I badly want to fuck it deeper into me. I want to feel it in my core.

But I'm not in control. It's all you and your alien comrades.

You keep up your teasing movements, bringing me right to the edge but never letting me go past it. "Note how the subject breathes faster, and cries out. It is difficult to decipher whether these cries are of pleasure or pain."

"Please, Zeta. *Please*," I murmur, but you ignore me, continuing to make clinical observations to your colleagues as blood throbs in my groin.

I give up any hope of being fucked to the hilt. You don't care about my satisfaction. I can't count the number of abductions when you haven't allowed me to come, but left me frustrated and needy. Perhaps this abduction will be like those.

Fine, then. I will suck as much pleasure out of this experience as I can, in spite of you.

I close my eyes and concentrate on the feeling of the probe sliding inside me, of my twitching muscles and racing heart, of the electricity pulsing through my nerves.

"And what will happen if we do this?" you say, slamming the probe deep into my ass, the cool handle pressed against my opening. I let out an incomprehensible shout.

I feel the five long fingers of each of your hands against my ass cheeks. Your thumbs must be holding the handle flush against my opening. You twist the probe ever so slightly. It's not enough movement. I need you to fuck me with it, here in front of all these alien eyes.

"Zeta, I need—"

"You do not *need*. Humans always say *need* when they mean *want*. They will remain an inferior race until they learn the difference."

I begin again, breathlessly. "Zeta, I want—"

You clasp a smooth, rubbery hand over my mouth, the other hand still holding the probe inside me. "What a human wants is none of our concern."

You keep your hand over my mouth as you continue to move the probe inside me, slowly and with no particular pattern. Sometimes you glide over my most sensitive spots, sometimes you twist, sometimes you wiggle the handle left and right to stretch my rim a little more. At one point, I feel one of your long, lubed fingers slide in with the wand.

You curl its smooth, spongy tip against my interior wall. I cry into your palm, keep crying as you brush the fingertip round and round, and then two fingertips, while the probe presses heavily against the opposite wall, stretching me deliciously. I start babbling into your hand: "Oh, Zeta, I like that, I like that, I like that—"

You lift your hand up enough to make sense of the words. "Explain, human."

"The stretch, and—*oh*—" My sentence dissolves into a wordless cry as Zeta gives the probe a full twist inside of me. I long to rub against my nipples, hard and peaked as they are. Why hasn't Zeta touched them yet, or shocked them? "I could come, Zeta, if you—"

"Do you *dare* command us?" Your shout fills my head, but the movement of the probe and your finger keeps its pace.

"No, Zeta, I just—" I pant. "Trying to help you understand the human sexual response."

"We understand enough to make you orgasm without instructions, puny human!" It sounds like the whole choir of aliens barking at me with their hollow, tinny voices. You slap your hand over my mouth again and my arousal bumps up a notch.

Your finger slips out and—*oh!*—the probe suddenly begins pulsing, vibrating. It starts with a soft, gentle rhythm, but each breath brings on a faster, stronger beat. You plunge the probe in and out of me—slowly at first and then faster, faster, until it's pounding into me. My insides feel like they're going to melt into one huge pool of come. My eyes roll around in my head and I take in your arm, your blank stare, and the few other faces I can see in my peripheral vision. I try to send telepathic messages to them. *Zeta's so good, really knows how to fuck me, Zeta should be a motherfucking hero on your planet, should be a hero on ours—*

I feel a sudden electric shock to my nipples, sharp like a needle prick. Then another, and another, until the quick succession turns into a steady, prickling buzz.

"Zeta, I'm close," I pant into your hand. "So close."

"We know." Your hollow voice somehow manages to sound smug. The others join in with a chorus of *we all know*s as you press against my swollen clit with your alien thumb.

My orgasm rumbles through me like a rocket launch.

You stay in character after I orgasm, but me—I start to lose focus. I'm a puddle of jelly. You have trouble getting the blindfold back on me with the head restraint still in place, so you unlock it. "Don't move," you say threateningly, but my neck's too wobbly to hold my head still, and it ends up rolling to the side. I find myself staring head-on into the eyes of the alien observer closest to me.

But it's not an alien. It's just a head—a statue

bust made from the same mold as your costume head, mounted on a heavy spring to allow movement.

I close my eyes and pretend I didn't see anything. Knowing how you did it doesn't reduce the bliss of just having come in front of a dozen or so voyeuristic Roswell grays.

You get the blindfold on me and unlatch the rest of the restraints. For the journey back to the couch, you carry me the whole way. Your rubbery skin is so smooth and flawless against mine. I wish I could spend my whole life as your guinea pig. "I love you, Zeta," I whisper as you lower to me to the couch. You chuckle.

It's the first time I've heard an alien laugh.

I fall asleep on the couch, and sometime later you're back—only it's *you* now, not Zeta. You're dressed in yoga pants and a tight white T-shirt. Your breasts are small and firm. I can see your nipples through the fabric.

I want to taste them.

I run my fingers through your hair and say, "Let's fuck."

You smile. "You're always so horny after you've been abducted by aliens."

"You usually are, too."

"What do you expect? Finding you naked on the couch, thinking about all those things Zeta does to you … it does a number on me." You slip your hand beneath the waistband of your yoga pants and move it around for a few moments before pulling it out to display an index finger wet with your arousal.

"Good," I say, climbing onto your lap. "Let me fuck you, then."

You smile and say something Zeta never would: "Your wish is my command."

Wordless Surrender

ALLIE COULDN'T ABIDE kneeling. She didn't need a sub who sat quietly at her feet, hoping to be petted and waiting for her command.

She had a service dog for that.

Moreover, it was burdensome to converse with someone whose mouth was next to her knees. Lip-reading from that position gave her a crick in the neck, and signing at such close proximity made it difficult to look at a person's face and also see what their hands were doing.

Bowing was another habit she trained out of her subs. Consent was important to her, and even when she wore hearing aids it was difficult to discern the difference between *yes* and *no* if she couldn't see the sub's lips. A sub who insisted on looking at the floor and not at her face when she gave directions didn't know the true meaning of surrender.

Marbeth, though—she was a sub through and through. For Marbeth, submission wasn't about playing a role. It was about turning over her expectations, habits and desires in order find a deeper truth.

Marbeth hadn't known a lick of sign language when Allie began working with her six months before. Now, simply because Allie had told her she should learn, she could carry on a full conversation without resorting to fingerspelling more than a few times. Sure, her movements had a stiffness and reserve that were the opposite of fluent, and sometimes she made facial expressions that inverted the meaning of the words she signed. But her willingness to learn and be corrected was beautiful. It reflected a capacity to yield in all things, to adapt to the will and pleasure of her keyholder.

Allie left her hearing aids untouched on her dresser as she prepared for Marbeth's visit. She opened the drawer where she kept new toys for her subs and pulled out a pair of leather handcuffs she'd purchased at the same time as Marbeth's collar, but never used. Each thick black strap had a stainless steel buckle on one end. Midway along its length a narrow, riveted band of leather held a shining steel ring. A short chain joined the ring of each cuff to the other, locked in place by a padlock matching the one on Marbeth's collar.

Allie pictured the cuffs against Marbeth's delicate wrists, dark bands slashing across pale skin. Arousal flushed through Allie's labia. Marbeth was beautiful in black: the grip of the collar around her elegant neck, the caress of cuffs around her slim ankles, the embrace of a silken scarf against her lips.

Allie had just pulled Marbeth's key from her jewelry box when Herman, the Boston terrier–spaniel mix who worked as her service dog, ran into the room and pressed his cold nose against her shin. She stroked his head to let him know he had her attention and, thus assured, he turned hightail to lead her to the front door.

Allie peered through the sidelight to find Marbeth on the stoop in a turquoise peplum raincoat that reached her knees. Allie froze for a moment, taken in by the view of her favorite pet. Marbeth was looking the other way, distracted perhaps by the sounds of the busy street behind her. She gazed off in the distance at something Allie could neither hear nor see, stroking her fingers self-consciously against her bare neck as if longing for the collar that wasn't yet around her throat.

Allie smiled, clutching the cool weight of the metal lock and key that hung on a steel chain around her wrist.

Inside the bedroom, removing Marbeth's raincoat was like unwrapping a gift. She wore nothing under the turquoise shell other than what Allie had commanded, and was all the more lovely for it. Her firm breasts—mounds of fresh cream dotted with caramel nipples—stood proudly over the red latex corset hugging her torso from lower ribs to hips, its black laces pulled snug to moderately restrict her breathing. The crotch of her negligible scarlet briefs was damp with arousal.

Allie hung the coat on a hook by the bedroom door, pulling the collar from its pocket as she did so. The leather was flexible and warm from Marbeth's body heat. Marbeth stepped closer, the exquisite scent of fresh skin mixed with citrus and cardamom wafting from her skin. She raised her chin, elongating and exposing her neck.

Allie brushed her fingers along the smooth skin, pausing over the carotid artery to feel Marbeth's pulse. Marbeth's lips parted slightly, her throat expanding as she sucked in a sharp breath.

Are you mine? The steel lock and key brushed against Allie's wrist as she signed the words.

Marbeth eyed it hungrily. *If you will have me.*

Allie latched the collar around Marbeth's throat. She removed the lock from the chain on her wrist and slipped it through the collar's buckle.

The expression on Marbeth's face became noticeably more relaxed the instant Allie locked it. The tension melted from her cheeks and the corners of her eyes. Her lower jaw dropped, letting go of its stranglehold on her upper teeth. Her breasts heaved as she took a shuddering breath, her lips quivering as the air passed through them. *I am yours, my Queen, and I live to serve you. Allow me to make you happy today.*

Allie smiled. *I have a surprise for you. Hold out your hands.*

Marbeth said nothing as she surrendered her hands to Allie, holding them palms up before her body. But her brows were question marks. She furrowed them the way people do in American Sign Language when asking, *Why?* She might as well have signed the word.

Because it pleases me, Allie answered.

Marbeth blushed—perhaps over embarrassment for asking a question without permission, or perhaps because pleasing Allie was her pleasure. Allie didn't worry about the reason. Instead, she took pleasure in how the blush made Marbeth's cheeks pink and darkened her lips. Allie wondered if Marbeth's labia were already the same shade of rose.

Allie removed the handcuffs from the drawer, leaving the chain and padlock that linked them behind for the moment. She set one in Marbeth's right palm as she looped the other around Marbeth's left wrist. Marbeth's eyes were heavy on her and she buckled it in place, and heavier as Allie proceeded to cuff her right wrist, as well.

Do you trust me? Allie signed.

Yes.

Allie turned back to the dresser to remove the chain and its padlock. They were cold. Allie clutched them to infuse her body heat into the metal before dropping both into Marbeth's open palms. Marbeth gulped. The lock over her throat swayed.

You understand what I want? Allie asked.

To bind my hands together. With her fingers clasped around the chain, Marbeth's words were clumsy and muffled. Still, Allie understood them.

You are very good at using words to communicate with me. But words aren't the only way to communicate. We must read each other's bodies and spirits as well—our breaths, our scents, the tension and relaxation of our muscles. The way each of us reacts to touch. I want to read you in a different way.

Marbeth's pupils grew wide and dark, encroaching on her irises until they were nothing but thin golden halos. She licked her lips.

Allie's plan for today was the right one.

She turned to the drawer and pulled out a large jingle bell that she immediately dropped to the floor. In an instant Herman was at her ankles, nudging her calves to get her attention, then nosing the bell to show her it had fallen. She patted him on the head and dismissed him, watching as his white tail disappeared behind the partially open bedroom door.

She picked up the bell and pressed it into Marbeth's palm beside the chain. *The bell is your safeword. Shake or drop it and I'll know to stop.*

Marbeth was as gorgeous as Allie had anticipated. She pressed a finger against the pale inside of Marbeth's left wrist. The blue veins that emerged from under the cuff seemed darker than usual, tracing runnels like sapphire rivers up Marbeth's palm. Allie pressed her thumb against the most prominent one. It pulsed under her touch, and Marbeth's breath quickened. Her nipples puckered into hard peaks.

Allie tugged at the chain that joined the two cuffs together. It was looped behind the central post of the headboard, the padlock securing it in place. Only Allie was capable of freeing Marbeth from her bondage. The thought made Allie quiver and her cunt gush. He labia grew slick, gliding against each other deliciously as she walked toward the foot of the bed to lock the ankle cuffs.

Is there anything you need to say before I gag you?

Marbeth shook her head and signed *no* with her captive right hand, the bell clasped firmly in her left. Her spread-open labia flushed ruby pink, glistening in the light from the overhead lamp.

No more signing after this. And no talking, either. Allie took the black scarf from its place under the pillow and held it in a straight line in front of Marbeth's mouth, and Marbeth opened willingly—such a sweet seduction, Marbeth's willingness. Allie couldn't help but press a kiss to Marbeth's lips, licking into the hot wet heat and feeling the vibrations of Marbeth's moan in her own cheeks for a tantalizing moment before pulling back. She slid the cloth across Marbeth's mouth and Marbeth let it fall between her teeth, clamping down on it eagerly as Allie pulled the fabric snug and tied it behind her head.

The blindfold came next, a simple satin sleeping mask to block out the light. Marbeth sank back into the pillow when Allie was done, the tightness of her neck and shoulders disappearing, her body going as soft as water, the way it always did at the moment Allie took complete power over her.

It was a power Allie strove to exercise wisely. Her plans for Marbeth this session were mild. She didn't need to push any sexual boundaries, only the boundaries of their trust. The pain toys were shut away in a drawer. Everything today was about primal pleasure unencumbered by words.

Allie removed the towel from the array of vibrators and dildos on the bedside table and slipped on a pair of black latex gloves. She chose a slim G-spot stimulator to start, coating it with lube before settling in between Marbeth's legs and drawing swirls across Marbeth's labia until the inner ones parted slightly—lips eager to be kissed. She pushed, feeling the resistance of Marbeth's muscles become acceptance as the device slid in, one inch and then another, then the acceptance transform into hunger as Marbeth's cunt actively pulled the final inches in. Marbeth clenched around the toy, arousal rippling through the muscles of her inner thighs.

Allie teased. She loved to tease—to turn the toy slowly this way and that, to drag it out a quarter inch only to push it right back in, to make small incremental movements that made Marbeth shiver with anticipation and hope for more. She loved watching Marbeth grow increasingly desperate, to see her breasts flush and her nipples grow dark, to place a hand on Marbeth's chin and feel her needy whines thrumming through muscle and bone.

Allie loved to tease, but she also loved to surprise.

She flicked the switch that made the toy vibrate.

Marbeth arched off the bed, her ribcage straining against her corset, her breasts jiggling sideways from the sudden movement. She rolled her hips in erratic circles that contrasted with Allie's more forceful thrusts.

Allie pressed her palm to Marbeth's flushed sternum, feeling her moans as percussive pulses before sliding up to her face, caressing her cheeks and the taut black cloth between her lips. Breath flared from Marbeth's nostrils onto Allie's thumb in hot, rapid puffs.

Her moans were growing, sending stronger tremors through her jaw and into Allie's fingers. It was similar to the feel of orchestral music through a speaker, though Marbeth's flesh made the vibrations warmer and more alluring, making them swell and recede like a tide.

When Marbeth arched again, her cry became a snare drum, sharp and rolling, against Allie's fingers. Wetness gushed from Marbeth's opening and onto the sheets below, soaking the room in her warm fragrance.

Allie checked Martha's pulse (quick but steady) and her breathing (an ecstatic staccato). There was no fear or dread in her pink cheeks or captive mouth. In her hand, the bell was still.

She was ready for more.

Allie pulled the toy out and selected a medium-sized kelly green dildo to use next. She didn't bother lubricating it. Marbeth's body was taking care of that need more than adequately. Allie's body wasn't doing bad, either. Wet arousal warmed her mound and inner thighs.

Marbeth continued to quake from her previous orgasm, but Allie was in no mood to wait. She plunged the phallus into Marbeth with a forceful swoop. Marbeth's hips lifted off the bed in a forceful counteraction. Her knuckles went pale as she gripped the bell in her left hand, her teeth clenching around the gag and the muscles in her pectorals and upper arms winding tight. Her gravity-flattened breasts went pert from the tension in her chest, her nipples sharp as mountain peaks. Allie couldn't resist pinching one.

Sexual contact immediately after an orgasm was always intense for Marbeth, the kind of intensity that Allie loved to play with. She enjoyed how wild Marbeth became, thrashing and moaning so violently Allie could feel echoes through the mattress and in Marbeth's twitching thighs. The grimace around Marbeth's gag looked almost pained as she fought the waves of sensation crashing through her body, as if she was afraid of drowning if she surrendered to them.

Allie rubbed the flats of her palms in small, steady circles against Marbeth's tense hips, willing her to give in to the pleasure. Marbeth's skin was covered in a fine sea spray of sweat, the sheen an irresistible temptation to Allie's tongue. She licked Marbeth's hip as she pulled the dildo slightly out, spinning it in a clockwise motion as she sank it slowly back in.

Marbeth trembled. Her labia and clitoris grew thicker with arousal. Her pulse throbbed against Allie's thumb where she held it at the juncture of Marbeth's hip and thigh.

Allie's own pulse pounded like a second heart between her legs.

Allie pulled the dildo out. It shone with Marbeth's wetness, glinting like an emerald in the light. Allie dragged it across Marbeth's pelvis, marking lines and nonsense letters into the skin just beneath the bottom hem of her corset. She traced it over the corset's laces—up, up, up to Marbeth's jiggling breasts, and drew lines around her areolas, astutely avoiding the hard nipples that so begged to be touched.

As Ally continued to tease Marbeth with the wet toy, she reached with her other hand for Marbeth's favorite: a lubricated eight-inch vibrator with a cervical stimulator and clitoral tongue. It was almost as thick as a small woman's fist, though not as large as Allie's. One day soon, they would work up to that. Marbeth's vagina would yield to Allie's hand, going pliant and snug around her, welcoming her on another intimate level.

Without preamble, Allie pressed the large vibrator to Marbeth's inner labia and watched it sink into her eager body, her lower belly visibly expanding as the toy ventured deeper. Marbeth's mouth fell slightly open around her cloth gag and her chest fluttered as if she was panting. Perhaps she was. Allie lifted her free hand and held it an inch from Marbeth's mouth, feeling her breath like humid gusts of summer wind.

With the vibrator in as far as it would go, Allie pressed the switch at its base. The toy buzzed in Allie's hand, the clitoral tongue lap-lapping against Marbeth's hard bud and the cervical stimulator covertly spinning inside her body. The bits of her cheeks that showed between gag and blindfold flushed from pink to hot pink to ruby red. Allie pressed her hand over Marbeth's throat, the collar bobbing as Marbeth swallowed, the vibrations of her vocal cords crescendoing more violently with each moan.

It wouldn't be long before Marbeth came again. The hand not clasping the bell wrapped around the center rail. The tendons in her wrist bulged. Her breaths were staccato heat, her arousal a musk that perfumed the air and hung in Allie's nostrils like desire. Tension coiled through Marbeth's muscles. She thrust herself onto the vibrator as hard as she could in her bound state, her ass cheeks clenching into tight knots, her lower belly going taut and rigid.

Allie slipped a gloved finger in alongside the vibrating toy, and Marbeth came, her vagina spasming as she lifted her hips off the bed—or rather, her hips lifted *her*. Their movement seemed to be completely beyond Marbeth's control.

Tears streamed onto Marbeth's cheeks from under her blindfold.

The bell stayed secure in her grasp.

Allie clicked off the toy and slid it from Marbeth's slick opening, setting it on the bedside table along with her gloves. Removing the steel chain from her wrist, she slipped the key into the lock joining Marbeth's wrists together.

Allie pushed the blindfold up to Marbeth forehead. *You may speak.*

Marbeth set the bell down on the pillow. Her eyes smiled. Her lips, still bound by the gag, struggled to join them. *Thank you. May I return the favor?* She paused, her eyes flicking down Allie's body.

You don't have to.

But I want to. I've been dreaming of eating you out for days.

Allie reached around Marbeth's head and untied the gag. She pulled off her panties and dropped them to the floor.

As she crawled up Marbeth's body to sink onto her face, she felt a hand grip her thigh. She looked into Marbeth's eyes. *What?*

Would you...? Marbeth glanced to the side, bashful.

You've been very good today. You may ask anything.

Marbeth bit her bottom lip. *Would you bind my hands again?*

Allie smiled. *It would be my pleasure.*

Books by Janelle Reston

To keep up with Janelle's latest releases, sign up for her readers' circle at *www.janellereston.com/readers-circle.* You'll get a free download, exclusive discounts, and the chance to participate in regular readers-only giveaways. You'll also be the first to know whenever she has a new book out!

Novels & Novellas

Tomboy

SOME KIDS' HEADS ARE in the clouds. Harriet Little's head is in outer space.

In 1950s America, everyone is expected to come out of a cookie-cutter mold. But Harriet prefers the people who don't, like her communist-sympathizer father and her best friend Jackie, a tomboy who bucks the school dress code of skirts and blouses in favor of T-shirts and blue jeans. Harriet realizes she's also different when she starts to swoon over Rosemary Clooney instead of Rock Hudson—and finds Sputnik and sci-fi more fascinating than sock hops.

Before long, Harriet is secretly dating the most popular girl in the school. But she soon learns that real love needs a stronger foundation than frilly dresses and feminine wiles.

Select Multi-Author Anthologies

Going Down: A House of Erotica Collection

Goodbye Moderation: Gluttony

To Obey Her: Femdom Erotica Stories

Find more anthologies at *www.janellereston.com/books*.

About Janelle Reston

JANELLE RESTON LIVES IN a northern lake town with her partner and their black cats. Her short stories have appeared in more than a dozen anthologies, including *Best Women's Erotica of the Year, Volume 2* and *Best Lesbian Erotica of the Year, Volume 2*. Her romance novella *Tomboy* was released from NineStar Press in 2018.

When Janelle's not writing, she enjoys gardening, birding, and binge-watching nature documentaries and sci-fi on Netflix.

Connect with Janelle and find her social media links at *www.janellereston.com*.

www.ingramcontent.com/pod-product-compliance
Lightning Source LLC
Chambersburg PA
CBHW031949130726
47904CB00012B/957